ALAN PLATER

The
Beiderbecke Affair

A Methuen P

First published in Great Britain in 1985
and reprinted 1987
by Methuen London Ltd
11 New Fetter Lane, London EC4P 4EE
Copyright © 1985 by Alan Plater
Front cover photographs © 1985
by Yorkshire Television Ltd
Printed in Great Britain by
Richard Clay Ltd, Bungay, Suffolk
Filmset by Northumberland Press Ltd,
Gateshead, Tyne and Wear

British Library Cataloguing in Publication Data

Plater, Alan
    The Beiderbecke affair.
    I. Title
    823′.914[F]   PR6066.L3

ISBN 0–413–57750–3 paperback

The Beiderbecke Affair

Also available
by Alan Plater
in Methuen Paperbacks

The Beiderbecke Tapes

For Bix

One

The school had been built during the 1960s and named after a councillor who had performed great service for the area. The voters, astute architectural critics all, re-named it San Quentin High within a week of the official opening by a smooth man from Whitehall with a sharp suit and a forward-facing haircut. He seemed under the impression that he was in either Bradford or Wakefield and such transgressions are not forgiven in the outer limits of Leeds. The consensus opinion afterwards was unanimous: the fellow was a hundred-carat prick, certain to go far. He did.

Twenty years on, San Quentin High continued to serve the growing estate round about, preparing young people for the great Job Centre of Life. There were regular pinnacles in the life of the school, and the greatest of these occurred on a daily basis, Monday to Friday, at four o'clock in the afternoon, when students and staff were allowed to go home.

On one such day, cold and grey with a hint of rain – a standard design for days in outer Leeds – Trevor Chaplin and Jill Swinburne crossed from the main escape hatch of the school to Trevor's van, a yellow vehicle carefully chosen from the GPO surplus range for its cheapness. Jill carried a pile of exercise books containing thirty-three essays about the relationship between Prince Hal and Falstaff, with the weary resignation of a time-served English teacher sure in the knowledge that twenty-nine of the essays would be of brain-shredding mediocrity, three would be illegible, and one would be brilliant, written by a bookmaker's son called Tristan, a regular winner of the Smartarse of the Year competition, and destined for Oxbridge, Whitehall and a forward-facing haircut.

Trevor carried no homework. Woodwork teachers have this advantage in life: you cannot reasonably carry thirty-three standard lamps home, even if you own a yellow ex-Post Office van. Trevor was preoccupied with thoughts of sex, and as they climbed into the van he said so, though the sexual content was not obvious:

'Do you realize this is our second anniversary?'

Jill gave no sign of having heard him.

Her apparent indifference did not worry Trevor. For the greater part of his forty years on the planet Earth he had been saying things that nobody took any notice of. One more example made little difference, and he climbed into the van, trying to remember which pocket his keys were in.

But they were observed. Mr Carter, history teacher and self-appointed cynical commentator on life's frail blossoms, was watching from the staffroom window. He adjusted his spectacles and murmured: 'Mrs Swinburne and Mr Chaplin grow more like an old married couple as the years drag by, don't you think?'

He turned to see that the staffroom was empty. He too was unworried, totally accustomed to saying things that made people walk away. He spoke in longer sentences than Trevor: that was the only difference.

Like the other members of staff, he was intrigued and marginally fascinated by the relationship between Jill Swinburne and Trevor Chaplin. Why should a bright, attractive young English teacher, with an apparently healthy concern for reputable causes like blue whales, battered wives, the nuclear menace and the Third World, spend so much time with a crumpled Geordie woodwork

2

teacher, whose passions were limited to jazz and association football? Lifts to and from school in a yellow van represented one level of human contact; communion of the flesh and spirit were another matter, especially the flesh. The majority view in the staffroom was that communion of the flesh had taken place, probably on a regular basis, and by God they wanted details.

Trevor knew the details. What chafed his soul were the implications.

As they drove to Jill's house, she suddenly reacted to his question in the playground.

'What was all that about our second anniversary?'

Trevor explained: 'It's two years and four months since your marriage broke up, and I started giving you lifts to school, and being supportive . . .'

She had taught him the word 'supportive'.

Jill finished the speech for him: 'And two years exactly since I dragged you into bed for the first time and slaked my lust on your body.'

Trevor nodded. It was true. That was the nagging anniversary. Like the song said, he remembered it well: a lift home in the van following a school production of *Joseph and His Amazing Technicolour Dreamcoat*, fish and chips with a bottle of Frascati in Jill's through-lounge, then a subtly-worded hint from the English Department to the Woodwork Department. Her precise words were: 'Do you fancy going to bed?' He did, and they did, and had continued to do so for the last two years, though they sometimes skipped the Frascati. It was the most exciting thing that had ever happened to Trevor Chaplin and he said so: 'It's the most exciting thing that ever happened to me . . .'

'What? Adventures under the duvet with Mrs Swinburne?'

'Yes. I thought at the time . . . life will never be the same again. And a year goes by, and then another year, and it's

3

all very much the same. Apart from the duvet. That gets better all the time.'

Jill smiled, a little cryptically. 'It's still awfully good for me, too, darling.'

Whenever she smiled and joked about sex, it bothered the hell out of Trevor. For the best part of forty years he had survived without talking about it, and certainly without joking about it. You sniggered about sex, muttered about it behind your hand, chalked on walls about it, but you never talked about it openly, when other people could hear you. Jill did so all the time. She talked about everything: sex, religion, politics and human relationships. These were all matters to be talked through, especially relationships. She was ruthless on relationships, and Trevor sometimes wanted to walk away, but that was not allowed.

He tried a traditional solution to the immediate problem.

'Let's go out and celebrate.'

'Like where?'

'We could go to a pub. Get drunk. If you want to hear some really bad New Orleans jazz, we could go to The Five Bells. Listen to Charlie Hardaker's Hot Seven.'

Jill shook her head.

'Sorry. I'm going to a Conservation meeting.'

Trevor shrugged. He usually shrugged about five hundred times a day. He might have guessed that on this sacred anniversary she would be out somewhere protecting the world's energy resources. That was something else she had taught him during the last two years: the world's energy resources were finite. He believed her. He even agreed with her that the resources should be protected. He just found it difficult to see how a small committee, most of whose members had beards, could have any practical impact on the world's major power-blocs.

He knew what she would say next.

4

'Why don't you come to the meeting?'

She knew he would refuse.

'I don't think so. I'm doing my bit for conservation. We're switching from standard lamps to table lamps. It's really 'cos of education cuts, but I reckon we'll have conserved a hundred acres of woodland by the end of term. Tell the committee. They'll be pleased.'

It was Jill's turn to shrug, but she was better at it than Trevor. Chaplin shrugs indicated resignation and defeat. Swinburne shrugs were radical and aggressive, making you feel ashamed for not fighting the good fight on behalf of trees, whales or whatever species was next on the agenda.

They travelled the last half-mile in an edgy silence, before the van pulled up outside Jill's house. She hated the house. It had been bought at the insistence of her ex-husband at a time when she still paid lip-service to loving, honouring and obeying. It was a coy architectural exercise in the executive-pixie style, part of an estate designed for the upwardly mobile. The men on the estate drove Volvos to the office, and wore cravats to the pub on Sundays. The women submerged their identities in their husbands' careers and drank coffee in each other's houses according to an unwritten rota system. The men and women all disapproved of Jill, who displayed CND posters in her window and allowed an itinerant woodwork teacher to park his yellow van outside the house all night, with neither shame nor public apology.

As Jill prepared to get out of the van, she suddenly turned to Trevor, with a quizzical look that indicated a question coming hard and painfully out of left field.

'Was there anybody before me? We've never discussed that. Any other duvets in your life?'

Trevor ducked behind his educated working-class jauntiness.

'Oh yes. I've had my share of emotional agony.'

Jill guffawed. When she laughed, she laughed loud, like a docker, another habit the neighbours found difficult to live with.

'You? Emotional agony!'

'Even woodwork teachers have emotions. I'm not made of teak.'

One of Trevor's occasional smiles drifted across his face, symptom usually of a bad joke or a guilty secret ready to pop out.

'What's so funny?'

Trevor lurched into the explanation: 'Mostly I manage with this amazing dream. I'm sitting there in the flat, listening to some music – Duke or Louis or Bix – the door opens and in walks this beautiful platinum blonde. I've always had this thing about blondes ... Kim Novak ... Grace Kelly ... Marilyn ...'

Jill instinctively touched her own hair, which the boot polish trade would have classified as dark tan.

'Forgive me my hair, Mr Chaplin.'

Trevor was eager to reassure her. In an average day he apologized almost as often as he shrugged. 'It's just a dream. I suppose you'd call it a sexual fantasy.'

Jill smiled, nodded and opened the door of the van, spilling six of the thirty-three exercise books. Trevor picked them up and handed them to her. As she made her way along the executive path leading to the front door, he called out, with a sudden attack of bravado: 'Hey! What happens if she shows up? There she is, the beautiful platinum blonde ... and the dream comes true and the earth moves ...'

Jill snapped back: 'That's easy. I scratch her eyes out. Yours too.'

She ignored the curious stare from a passing jogger – this was jogging country – as she unlocked her front door, still surprised by the venom of her own reaction. It did not become a free-thinking independent woman to be jealous of an imaginary platinum blonde. She sat down on the Habitat studio couch in the executive through-lounge and dumped the exercise books on the floor. She was as puzzled as her staffroom colleagues by her relationship with Mr Chaplin. He had strange obsessions about long-forgotten footballers and deceased jazz musicians, obsessions she had no ability to share. She had tried, and had even learned names like Jacky Milburn and Art Blakey, but which one played football and which one had a band she could never be sure. But Trevor Chaplin was gentle, he made her smile, and probably thought machismo was a kind of pasta or a goalkeeper. They found cause to giggle under the duvet, and that was something to cherish.

She got up and marched into the kitchen recess to make a healthy salad of the sort Trevor hated, a little concerned that she might be going soft on the male of the species.

A panoramic sweep across the urban landscape of the mighty Leeds conurbation at night could easily lead to confusion with San Francisco, if there were a bridge, Rome, if there were a Vatican, or Athens, given an Acropolis and a whiff of lapsed glory. In the blackness, the sub-standard housing and empty factories disappear, and the lights shining out, from street-lamps and buses, public houses and filling-stations, police cars and off-licences, seem like beacons of hope in a hostile world. They are not, but they look like it.

Trevor Chaplin's attic flat, perched on top of a crumbling Victorian pile in a once-prosperous suburb whence the textile merchants had long since fled, commanded just such an impressive view of the pretty, nocturnal sprawl. He never looked at it. Once at home, he would climb inside a pair of headphones and listen to jazz.

As a teenager, he had tried and failed to play guitar like Django Reinhardt, saxophone like Charlie Parker, or trumpet like Louis Armstrong.

Eventually he had come to terms with the reality of his condition: he was better at woodwork. By way of compensation, he filled his head with music nightly, and the walls of his flat with record shelves.

On the night in question, and it was a night destined to be called into question, he was filling his head with Bix Beiderbecke when the red light flashed. The red light was a result of complaints from his friends, most of them Jill Swinburne, that he never answered his front door when he was buried inside his headphones. His response was to buy some wire and a lamp from the neighbourhood do-it-yourself store, and create a primitive but effective early warning system, so that when somebody rang his doorbell, the red light flashed, and however deeply interred he might be in Basie or Ellington, he would emerge to answer it. It was a cumbersome sledgehammer to crack a very modest nut but that was often the Chaplin style.

Trevor observed the red light flashing, removed his headphones, switched off the record with an apology to Bix, and crossed to the front door of his flat, which opened directly into the room. For all practical purposes, like living in it, the room was the flat and vice versa.

He opened the door and stared. Framed in the doorway was a dazzlingly beautiful platinum blonde. He reacted like any Geordie of pure birth: 'Whyebuggerman!'

Clearly, the dazzlingly beautiful platinum blonde was not familiar with the verbal peculiarities of the North-East. 'You what?'

Trevor's excitement sagged a little: if her accent was from LA it was more likely Lower Attercliffe than Los

8

Angeles. He stumbled into a quick apology: 'Sorry. It's an old North Country expression indicating that I'm mildly astonished.'

'What is there to be astonished about?'

He decided valour was a better bet than discretion: 'You might be offended, but you're a beautiful platinum blonde.'

She smiled a toothpaste commercial smile, and tinkled a West Riding laugh with only a hint of Woodbines in its texture.

'I'm not offended by that. Can I come in?'

Trevor stood aside, restrained himself from bowing, and watched as she drifted across the room, as if walking on castors. She wore a heavy-duty winter coat, in recognition of the climate, but the sway of the hips gained in impact by the element of concealment. She sat down, uninvited but sure of her welcome, in his favourite armchair: in truth, the only armchair.

Then she dug into a large holdall, and produced the mail order catalogues.

'Would you like to buy something?'

Trevor's fantasy, frayed by her accent, decomposed totally at the sight of the mail order catalogues.

'You're selling things from mail order catalogues?'

'Yes. What did you think I was here for?'

This was the sort of question he found difficult to answer, simply because he knew the answer. He thought she was there to carry him to previously uncharted peaks of ecstasy and sexual perception, but he also realized that was certainly the wrong answer to her question. He browsed through the catalogues with polite apathy, fifty pages at a time, then handed them back.

'Sorry, love, but I don't buy things from mail order catalogues. Come to think of it, I very rarely buy anything at all.'

This was obviously difficult for a dazzlingly beautiful platinum blonde to come to terms with.

'You must buy something. What about clothes?'

'Do I look as if I buy clothes?'

Trevor was subjected to an offhand scrutiny, followed by a succinct conclusion: 'See what you mean.' Then her eyes scanned the walls of the flat. 'Did you steal all them records?'

'Of course not. I bought them, with genuine coins of the realm.'

She brandished the portliest of the catalogues in his direction. 'Have a look at page six hundred and fifty-nine.'

Trevor did as he was told and found what he expected and feared: Mickey Mouse records, mostly devoted to singing along with aged stars of 1950s television programmes, golden greats of light opera, the pipes and drums of obscure Scottish regiments and an assortment of Al Jolson hits played by a banjo band. Trevor returned the catalogue.

'Sorry. I only collect jazz records.'

This statement of musical philosophy made up her mind about Trevor's place in the great scheme of mail order consumerism.

'My Uncle Edwin collected jazz records. He was round the twist.'

Trevor nodded. He could well believe it. She replaced the mail order catalogues in her bag, stood up and crossed to the door, murmuring as she did so: 'I'm sorry you feel this way about the Cubs.'

'What are you talking about? Cubs? You mean little Scouts?'

'Yes. I'm only doing this to raise money for the Cubs football team. They need a set of shirts and some corner flags.'

Trevor Chaplin, being a kind man, who had been a Cub in his time, and a member of many football teams, was touched and moved. He delved into the back pocket of his jeans.

'That's different. Let me give you a donation. That's assuming you can't get me the sort of records I want . . .'

'Tell me what sort of records you want, and I'll tell you if I can get them for you.'

Her attitude softened, as if his back-pocket gesture indicated a degree of generosity and sanity placing him in a different category from poor mad Uncle Edwin. She quickly discovered that inviting Trevor Chaplin to talk about jazz records was akin to asking the Pope for a quick rundown on original sin. She resumed her place in the armchair while Trevor made a cup of tea and explained about his latest musical obsession, Bix Beiderbecke. Had she been paying proper attention, she would have learned that Beiderbecke, the first great white jazz musician, was born at Davenport, Iowa, in March 1903, drank himself to death and joined the great big band in the sky in August 1931, at the age of twenty-eight. It was said that Bix's playing sounded like bullets shot from a bell and the essential point of the lecture was that a four-LP set of his records, currently available, would make Trevor Chaplin's world complete.

The dazzlingly beautiful platinum blonde noted the details, winced as she drank her sugarless tea, accepted ten pounds in cash and assured Trevor that the records would be delivered within twenty-four hours or he would be given his money back. She handed him a receipt as a guarantee of good behaviour, then left.

Trevor, still unable to believe the evidence of his senses, broke the habit of a lifetime and looked out of his window. He saw his blonde visitor met at the gate by a huge man, the size and texture of a mature Pennine hill. They climbed on bicycles and rode off into the night. Trevor turned away from the window, and thus did not see a man called Harry taking a dog called Jason for a walk along the street.

Next morning, according to the custom and practice of the last two years and four months, Trevor Chaplin collected Jill Swinburne in his yellow van, ready for another day devoted to educating the young in all that is finest in our island heritage.

Jill had some exciting news to share: 'I was adopted last night.'

'I didn't even know you were an orphan.'

'As a candidate. I'm going to stand for the Council in the by-election. Jill Swinburne, your Conservation candidate.'

The by-election had been called when Councillor Purvis, a disillusioned Tory, decided to join the SDP. As he was crossing the High Street from the Conservative Club to the Alliance committee room, housed behind a pork butcher's, he was struck a mortal blow by a brewery truck. It was generally agreed that it was an appropriate death for Councillor Purvis, and typical of the strange quirks that control the political development of the nation. Outside of his immediate family, nobody missed him very much. Underneath a brewery truck was probably his true level in the scheme of things, and whoever won the by-election would certainly produce a great leap forward in diction, literacy and the ability to stand unaided during the daylight hours.

Trevor was delighted to hear Jill's news: 'Hey, that's great!' And then he was nervous: 'Does that mean we have to go knocking on doors, giving out leaflets, canvassing, all that stuff?'

He knew the answer already.

'We shall need willing volunteers with reliable yellow vans and I put your name down.'

'Thanks.'

12

They drove on in silence, pondering approaches to the democratic process, before Trevor revealed his exciting news: 'You'll never guess what happened to me last night.'

'Easy. The door of your flat opened and in walked a beautiful platinum blonde.'

'Yes.'

There was another, shorter silence, as they pondered approaches to the erotic fantasies of Geordie woodwork teachers living alone, and in exile. As usual, Jill was less inhibited and more adept with the sexual verbals: 'Don't tell me. The pianist played "As Time Goes By" and you looked into each other's eyes and made passionate love on the tigerskin rug.'

'No. I bought some Bix Beiderbecke records in aid of the Cubs football team.'

Jill did not believe her version of the story, but she did not believe his version either. Trevor was always embarrassed when he was caught out telling the truth, and they were still arguing as they arrived at school. She refused to let him carry her thirty-three exercise books.

As they made their way to the air-lock separating education from the world, she snapped at him: 'Beautiful blondes do not go from door to door selling from mail order catalogues. You are a very conventional man, Mr Chaplin, but there are times when I think you're round the bend.'

'Like her Uncle Edwin,' muttered Trevor, then immediately regretted it.

Their little local difficulty was observed on high by Mr Carter from the staffroom window.

'Domestic strife. I can spot it at a hundred paces. Even money says the earth didn't move last night.'

He looked around the staffroom for takers. He saw teachers of all ages, one-third of them with punk hairstyles, variously blowing up footballs, looking for better jobs in the *Times Ed Supp* and desperately swotting up the wisdom they were scheduled to hand on in the first lesson. They all ignored him. It was the tradition of San Quentin High: everybody talked and nobody listened.

Mr Carter was unconcerned. He wanted to talk to Trevor Chaplin, whom he greeted with uncharacteristic warmth: 'Just the man I'm looking for! I have a technical problem.'

'Try the Samaritans,' suggested Jill.

Mr Carter pointed to an area of floor, strewn with pieces of metal and plastic. Trevor inspected them with the same gusto he might have applied to Homer's *Odyssey*. He asked the obvious question: 'What is it?'

Mr Carter explained: 'When these are properly assembled, I will be able to trim my hedges and verges in less than half the time it takes manually. You behold an electrical hedge and verge trimmer. However ...' He picked up a sheet of instructions and wafted them towards Trevor: 'The instructions appear to be in some form of Japanese, and I need an experienced woodwork teacher to help me, as a gesture of friendship and professional loyalty.'

Trevor doubted the premise but read the first instruction: 'Applicate the component A to bracket B with appropriate screwing.'

Jill laughed. Trevor returned the instructions to Mr Carter. 'As an experienced woodwork teacher, I recommend you take it back to the shop.'

Mr Carter would not be moved.

'I didn't buy it from a shop. I bought it at the door.'

Trevor and Jill exchanged looks, whiplash fashion, like a pair of Wimbledon seeds trading volleys at the net.

'The door?' asked Trevor.

'Yes,' said Mr Carter, 'from what I can only describe as a dazzlingly beautiful platinum blonde.'

'In aid of the Cubs football team?' suggested Jill.

Mr Carter smiled and nodded.

Trevor rushed to the door, yelling: 'Howay the lads!'

As he closed the door behind him, thirty-three exercise books full of glib and shallow thoughts about Falstaff and Prince Hal landed where, seconds earlier, his head had been.

At the end of the school day, Trevor Chaplin walked from the woodwork room to the staffroom, clutching a fully-assembled hedge and verge trimmer. To do this, he had to go up some stairs and down some stairs, even though both rooms were on the same floor. The school had been designed in accordance with the design philosophy then in vogue at the Ministry of Education, which was based on the theory that arduous and complicated journeys from A to B create initiative in the young.

Trevor marched into the staffroom and presented the machine to Mr Carter, who had just given up on the *Times* crossword since he could only think of a dirty answer to the 17 Across anagram. He grasped the machine with the eagerness of one who has paid hard cash.

'Mr Chaplin, I am deeply indebted for the years of work and loving dedication that you have given to this –'

Trevor interrupted him: 'I didn't do it. I handed the problem to the lads in Three B, as a project.'

Fear and panic flooded Mr Carter's eyes.

Trevor reassured him: 'Don't worry. I didn't tell them it was for you. Mind you, there is a small problem.'

He explained the problem. The manufacturers had only supplied three feet of electric cable. He assumed that the gardens in Taiwan were on the small side.

Mr Carter was unconcerned by the brevity of the flex. His eldest son, now married and selling computer software

15

in the Midlands, had left behind many miles of extension leads. It was technically possible to hoover the house across the road or have a mains-operated shave in the pub around the corner. He had done neither, but the capability existed. He was profoundly grateful to Mr Chaplin for his good works and kindness of heart.

Jill walked in on the display of gratitude, carrying thirty-three exercise books containing thirty-three essays explaining why, in Five A's own words, they wouldn't buy a second-hand car from Mark Antony. She was startled by the unusual display of warmth directed at Trevor by Mr Carter.

'What have you been doing to make him say thank you?'

'I assembled his hedge trimmer. At least, I got Three B to assemble his hedge trimmer.'

'But he didn't tell them it was for me,' said Mr Carter, as he saw the alarm in her face.

'Take me home,' said Jill. 'I want to make an improper suggestion in the van.'

Mr Carter, clutching his hedge trimmer, watched the van leaving the school grounds, pondering the nature of Jill's suggestion, wishing he were a party to it and lamenting his lost adolescence.

Jill's suggestion was deceptively vague: 'Do you fancy going out tonight? Belated anniversary celebration?'

Trevor sniffed several possible rats.

'What is it? Save the whale or single-parent families?'

'I've got no kids. I can't be a single-parent family.'

'Have you considered fostering a blue whale? Solve two problems –'

'Knock it off, smartarse! Do you want to help deliver five thousand leaflets to the voters? Vote for Swinburne, your Conservation candidate.'

She held up a sample leaflet. He gave it a token squint

but reserved most of his attention for the semi-rush-hour traffic. He had nothing against the environment but suspected that dumping five thousand leaflets on innocent voters would be dead boring. He would rather go to his flat and carry out essential maintenance, like buying a bag of sugar and cutting his toe-nails.

Jill was clearly expecting an answer: 'Well?'

'Well,' echoed Trevor, 'you've always told me to be honest about my true feelings.'

'Go on then, be honest.'

'It sounds dead boring, and I'd rather buy a bag of sugar and cut my toe-nails.'

It was not a good thing to say. They drove on in a silence that would have resisted a Texas chain-saw.

Two hours later, Jill had taken several giant steps in the democratic process. Five thousand leaflets were neatly stacked in piles of one hundred across the length and breadth of the executive through-lounge. At that precise moment, the front door opened and in came Trevor, accompanied by a blast of mad March gale that operated locally on an all-the-year-round franchise, scattering leaflets in gay and random profusion. Jill Swinburne was not pleased.

'Sorry,' said Trevor, sensing it was not enough. 'The door was unlocked, so I came in,' he added, knowing it was still not enough. 'I thought I might help you deliver some leaflets,' he threw in, hoping that might be just enough.

'Has cutting your toe-nails lost its glamour? Or did your beautiful platinum blonde not show up?'

'Yes and no.'

He showed her a flat, square cardboard box and told how it had been waiting for him, leaning against the door of the flat on his return home from school. All the outward evidence suggested it contained four Bix Beiderbecke records, but it was adorned with several layers of Sellotape and –

Jill interrupted the meandering explanation: 'And you can't unwrap it?'

Trevor smiled. 'I knew you'd understand. It's all stuck up with tape and you've got better fingernails than me, and I can't find my scissors. That's what I like about you. You never lose the scissors.'

'I always knew I had that extra-special something,' said Jill as, true to her image, she found the scissors in two-point-five seconds. Trevor trampled through election leaflets to the studio couch, and was on the brink of a sitting position when Jill struck the deal.

'I'll unwrap your parcel while you sort out those leaflets in neat piles of one hundred.'

He dropped to his knees and started work. It was almost as exciting as buying sugar, and on a par with cutting his toe-nails. He had almost completed one neat pile of a hundred leaflets by the time Jill penetrated the Sellotape. He wanted to grab the records from her, rush home and play them all night, but for diplomatic reasons concentrated very hard on making a second pile of a hundred leaflets.

'What records did you order?'

'Four LPs by Bix Beiderbecke.'

'Try not to cry on the carpet.'

She held up the records for him to see, one at a time. They were An Evening with Wolfgang Amadeus Mozart, Living Legends of the Cinema Organ, The George Formby Songbook, Volume Three and Everyday Spanish for Beginners. Trevor abandoned his democratic piles to have a close look.

'That's wrong. They're not even nearly the right records. Somebody must have made a mistake.'

Jill kissed him gently on the forehead, like a mother consoling a child.

'You made the mistake, sweetheart. Look not upon the blondes when they are platinum.'

The suburb inhabited by Mr Carter and others of his ilk was jerry-built in the 1930s by a speculator who had spent his honeymoon in the Lake District and took his revenge by naming the avenues, closes and crescents after the better-known beauty spots. Windermere flowed into Ullswater, Coniston dribbled into Derwent, and overall unity was achieved because all the houses were semi-detached and identical, not so much stockbrokers' Tudor after the manner of the Home Counties, but acting bank managers' mini-baronial, which had cunningly anticipated the style of Lego.

Mr Carter lived at 41, Ullswater Close, distinguished from its neighbours by neglect. Being a historian, he took a broad view of property maintenance. He argued that if history began millions of years ago when scaled creatures dragged themselves from the primeval slime, and was destined to end at some unspecified date in the future by act of God or president, it did not matter a damn if the stucco on his bay window was unstuck, or the hedges and verges of the back garden were untrimmed. His attitude towards the latter had changed dramatically with the arrival of the dazzlingly beautiful platinum blonde, and now, thanks to the good offices of Trevor Chaplin, Three B and his son's extension leads, he was about to restore his privet to a proper state of suburban grace.

He placed the hedge trimmer on the ground close to the hedge and plugged the flex into the socket of an extension lead. He walked along the extension lead until he arrived at its plug, which he placed in the socket of a second extension lead. The flex of the second extension lead trailed across the back yard, up the wall and through the open kitchen window.

Mr Carter went into the kitchen, and inserted the plug of the second extension lead into the socket normally used for the cooker. He peered from the window to inspect his work and concluded that it was good. He murmured a quiet blessing, safe in the knowledge that his wife was at her evening class in Elementary Archaeology and there was nobody present to trample on his daydreams.

'I hereby declare my trimmer operative and may the Lord bless all those hedges which are made glorious by her.'

He switched the power on in the kitchen.

There followed four small explosions. The hedge trimmer blew up first and was followed, at equal intervals, by each of the electrical junctions in the garden, and, a little more loudly, by the power point in the kitchen.

At that moment, Trevor Chaplin and Jill Swinburne were delivering election leaflets, walking in parallel either side of Coniston Avenue. Trevor called across: 'Did you hear four small explosions?'

Jill shook her head. 'No, I don't think so.' And she continued delivering to the odd numbers.

Trevor shrugged. 'In that case, neither did I.'

The morning after the small explosions, there was a large explosion. Trevor was in the woodwork room, brooding on the latest education cuts, and the feasibility of kids making one table lamp between three, when Mr Carter stormed in and shouted at him: 'Chaplin! I want a word with you about Three B and their hedge-trimming project!'

He gesticulated with his right hand, like a dictator in training, and Trevor could not help noticing that the hand was heavily bandaged, from fingertip to upper wrist.

'Did something,' he asked gently, 'go wrong?'

Mr Carter explained, with articulate hysteria, that he had been switching on the power to bring his hedge trimmer to life when there were four small explosions, the final one in the series causing considerable damage to his hand. Trevor smiled, as he realized he had won a small victory.

'Was this about twenty past seven last night?'

'Yes.'

'I knew I was right! I did hear four small explosions!'

Mr Carter indicated that he was not impressed by Trevor's memory: that he held him totally responsible for the state of his hand: that he expected him to do something about the defective hedge trimmer: that he would also appreciate the immediate deportation of Three B and their woodwork teacher to Van Diemen's Land. Trevor's offer to slip out across lunchtime for a bunch of grapes did little to ease his anguish.

He slammed the door on exit, causing great excitement among a group of sixth formers researching into earth tremors on the floor above, Mr Carter registering several points on their Richter scale.

Driving home after school that evening, Trevor took the wrong turning. Jill noticed immediately.

'You've taken the wrong turning.'

'I need to check something out.'

'You need to take me home.'

He handed her a piece of paper. It was the receipt given to Trevor by the blonde and on it was written an address: Sunset Mail Order Supplies, 27, Aristophanes Street. She handed it back.

'I want to go home.'

Trevor reacted sharply, by the standards of one whose normal demeanour was on a par with that of the average spaniel.

'I feel responsible for the fact that Mr Carter's hand looks like an Egyptian mummy. I also feel pissed off that I paid ten quid for some Bix Beiderbecke records and the wrong ones turned up. Aristophanes Street is the only clue we have. Aristophanes Street must be checked out.'

Jill, stunned by this sudden display of resolution, decided to sit back, think of the Empire or an equivalent, and be driven to Aristophanes Street. In any case, she was confident that there was no such street, outside of downtown Piraeus.

She was wrong. Five minutes later, the van turned a corner, and on the wall there lingered a sign that read Aristophanes Street. Nothing beside remained. The demolition squad had recently departed, leaving behind a still-smouldering bonfire and a desolate, brick-littered plain, boundless and bare. Where once kids had larked, dogs had peed, drunks had sung of Nelly Dean, and people had talked about the latest trouble at the mill, a dusty and drowsy numbness hung upon the air.

Trevor and Jill got out of the van to look more closely at the space that was recently Aristophanes Street.

Trevor muttered: 'It won't be easy, finding number twenty-seven.'

'Not easy.'

'If you're elected to the Council, you won't do this sort of thing, will you?'

She placed a reassuring hand on his shoulder. 'We're against demolition. We're against practically everything.'

Trevor was into a deep seam of harsh Geordie nostalgia. 'There's a lot of this where I come from.'

He sighed a sigh that started somewhere in the heart of the industrial revolution, then opened the door of the van.

'I want to go home.'

Jill had assumed that the trauma of Aristophanes Street would quell Trevor's lust for investigation, but she was wrong. As he stopped outside her house, he emerged from a long and brooding silence.

'Cubs football teams!'

She decided to ignore him, but he repeated the statement while they were eating one of her speciality salads: what Trevor usually called 'nuts and two kinds of lettuce', except this time he ate the food without insulting it first, and then said: 'Cubs football teams!'

'Why do you keep saying that?'

'I bought some records and Mr Carter bought a hedge trimmer, at the door, from a beautiful platinum blonde . . .'

Jill applied her best blondes-are-bloody-boring face but Trevor plunged on, in a concentrated bout of frowning deduction.

'. . . In both cases, we were told the money was in aid of the Cubs football team, to buy shirts and corner flags.'

He sat back, chewing reflectively on a stick of celery. He made his final judgement.

'We have to check out the Baden-Powell connection.'

'Eat your celery and shut up.'

'It's fabulous, this salad . . . I can feel it doing me good.'

While they were washing up, Jill poured a jug of water over his head by way of punishment for the remark. When his shirt was dry, they set out to deliver more leaflets.

This time their chosen patch was fractionally upmarket from Mr Carter's precinct, a private estate thrown together in the 1950s by a builder whose real ambition was to win the Open Golf Championship; hence the avenues, closes and crescents had names like Sandwich, Hoylake and Troon. Trevor explained the significance of the names as they tramped the pavements and verges. Jill thought Sandwich, Hoylake and Troon sounded more like a firm of lawyers, but conceded that she was no lover of organized professional sport, and on the whole found more excitement in picking fluff out of pockets.

Few of the houses had numbers. Most of them had names – Muirfield Mansion, Bunkered and Chez When – plus labradors and burglar alarms. From such a house emerged the Baden-Powell connection.

Trevor saw the Cub immediately and called out to Jill: 'I'll see you back at the van.'

Jill was deep in a discussion about seal-culling with a man who was out checking his fences and dusting his Jaguars. She scarcely noticed Trevor's departure.

It could easily be argued that Trevor was not sensible. A man, albeit law-abiding and a fully paid-up member of the NUT, following a uniformed Cub, aged ten and weighing in around sixty pounds, along leafy lanes and tree-shrouded paths in an English suburb is likely to be regarded with suspicion. The fact that the man is relatively normal, with healthy giggles under a duvet to prove it, does little to reassure the mean-minded and the sceptical.

Such thoughts were far from Trevor's mind. He was victim of a simple equation: a Cub implied a pack, a pack implied a football team, and a football team implied a platinum blonde raising money for corner flags. His nose was in the tramlines and he was going to the depot.

He followed the Cub, at a discreet distance, along a path and through a churchyard, as far as a neat, brick-built hut. The boy went in. Trevor waited, pondered and acted.

He walked into the hall as the boys were reaching the climax of their Grand Howl. In piercing chorus they yelled: 'We will do our best!'

Then the ancient ritual petered out as the pack and their

24

leader, a young woman professionally known as Akela, became aware of Trevor standing by the door, doing his best to look natural, relaxed and unlurking. Akela, who had been advised to get out and meet people to conquer her natural timidity, and had assumed that running a Cub pack would match the specification, gurgled an incoherent syllable. Trevor attempted a reassuring smile.

'Good evening. I'm sorry to interrupt you in the middle of your dob dobs but –'

Akela found words. 'Are you a parent or an official of the Scouts Association?'

'No.'

'In that case, I must ask you to leave. We've had a lot of trouble with prowlers in the area and –'

Trevor reacted sharply to the accusation. 'I'm not a prowler! I just want to know if you lads have got a football team.'

Mention of football caused a stir among some of the cubs, one of whom tapped Akela on the arm.

'I'll handle this,' he said.

'Thank you, Simon,' replied his tribal chief, in a quivering whisper.

Simon walked across to Trevor and stared up at him. He was a sturdy nine-year-old and his eyes carried the fragile innocence of a puff adder. Trevor was disturbed by Akela's confidence in the boy, let alone Simon's confidence in himself. Confidence of any kind he found alarming, especially among the young.

'Football, you say? Yes. We had a football team.'

'Had?'

'We were chucked out of the League for bringing the game, and the Cubs, and the memory of Baden-Powell, into disrepute.'

Trevor could not help smiling. It could again be argued that he was not sensible.

'Disrepute? How did you do that?'

Simon smiled back at him. 'Like this!'

He gave Trevor a mighty kick on the shins, causing him to drop the leaflets, so that he could clutch the pain with all available hands. Akela began screaming, the boys started to shout and stomp while Simon towered menacingly under Trevor's nose.

'Next question?' he asked.

Trevor sat by where the fireside would have been if executive-style houses did not come ready-supplied with gas central heating. He had his trouser-leg rolled up and his foot in a bowl of water while Jill bathed the ferocious bruise on his shin.

'Didn't I tell you to be prepared?'

'No.'

'Sorry. I intended to.'

She kissed him gently and affectionately on the bruise.

'Better?'

'A bit better.'

Again she kissed the bruise, then looked up at him, with an expression comprising equal parts sweetness, compassion and lust.

'Did he kick you in any other places?'

'I don't think so,' said Trevor, thoughtfully, 'but it might be sensible to check.'

He whistled four bars of 'As Time Goes By'. Jill stood up and threw him a towel.

'Dry your foot. I'll slip out to the shed for the tigerskin duvet.'

It was a warm night and they made love on and around rather than under the duvet, trading smiles and confessions, sharing tiny throbs and twitches, laughing quietly with each other.

'Funny,' said Jill, 'how our life keeps falling open at this page.'

'I have a question, Mrs Swinburne.'

They shuffled and readjusted. Trevor asked his question.

'If women have more erogenous zones than men ...'

She had taught him the phrase 'erogenous zones', with inventive illustration, four months into their relationship, once they realized it was ongoing, inevitable and fun.

'Go on with your question, Mr Chaplin.'

'It isn't easy if you're doing that. But don't stop.'

She did not stop, and with phenomenal self-discipline, Trevor completed his question.

'If women have more erogenous zones than men, why didn't God give men more hands?'

'There is no God. That's why I have to manage with you.'

They managed, happily, with each other. Suddenly Trevor laughed, loud and uninhibited.

'Hey up, petal, here come the asterisks!'

The bedroom was awash with asterisks, waves lashed on a rocky sea-shore, thunder roared, lightning flickered around the duvet, and the sixth form's Richter scale registered a magnitude of earth tremor hitherto unknown to the scientific mind.

Afterwards, Trevor said: 'And afterwards they slept.'

'Didn't you tell me in the great days of music hall and variety it was always twice-nightly?'

'Variety is dead.'

'Don't you believe it,' said Jill.

She fell fast asleep.

Mr Carter was quick to spot their blissful hangover next morning in the staffroom.

'Mrs Swinburne, you are glowing like the vital morn. And even Mr Chaplin has a blush upon his damask cheek.'

'Carbolic,' said Trevor.

'Are you planning to spoil it?' asked Jill, who had sniffed an air of privileged information hovering behind Mr Carter's joviality.

'Yes. The headmaster would like to see you, Mr Chaplin.'

'Golly!' said Jill. 'Old Chappers is up before the beak!'

'Immediately was the message,' added Mr Carter, as Trevor reacted to the news from high authority by scratching his shin and making a cup of coffee.

'Bollocks.'

Ten minutes later, Trevor set out on the overland trail from the staffroom to the study of the headmaster, Mr Wheeler. The teachers and students of San Quentin High were unanimous about their headmaster. Noble was not the first word that came into their minds; shifty – that was the first word, closely followed by others, like spineless and deluded. His main delusion lay in his self-esteem, clearly wasted on such a self. He looked in the mirror while shaving and saw a latter-day Mr Chips, with the bonus of organizational flair. The opinion within the school was that the only resemblance to Mr Chips was a hint of greasiness, a feeling that somebody had been too generous with the vinegar and an agreement that they would willingly say goodbye to him at five minutes notice, any day of the week, and throw in fifty pence for a leaving present.

Outside Mr Wheeler's room was a bell-push and a panel of coloured lights, rumoured to have fallen off the back of a tram-car on Blackpool promenade. Beside the lights were several paragraphs of written instructions explaining what course of action the bell-pusher should adopt in relation to the possible colour combinations. Trevor had never read these instructions. His method was to wait two minutes for the green light to go on. In the absence of a green light, he would wander back to the woodwork room, assuming that a second summons would arrive sooner or later – he had never been to see Mr Wheeler voluntarily – unless the immediate crisis gave way to a greater disaster, which it generally did.

This time the green light flashed promptly. Trevor was unworried by this unusual spurt of efficiency. He guessed the news would be of further education cuts, and a suggested policy shift from table lamps to leadless pencils or balsa-wood bookmarks.

He was wrong. Mr Wheeler sat behind his desk, perfecting his image, while in the corner of the room stood a tall, fair-haired young man, wearing a suit that fitted, and with a haircut that showed signs of facing forward.

Mr Wheeler peered at Trevor across a hundred-year gap in understanding. Trevor knew this man had never been near a duvet and was incapable of giggling, whatever the circumstances. Today, Trevor Chaplin was invulnerable.

'Mr Chaplin ... Mr Hobson.'

This was obviously an introduction.

'Pleased to meet you, Mr Hobson.'

Trevor held out an amiable right hand, which the young man ignored.

'To be precise, Sergeant Hobson,' he said, with a gentle emphasis on the rank.

'And tell Mr Chaplin what you told me,' added Mr Wheeler, always quick to see the most profitable direction in which to crawl.

'Sergeant Hobson, BA.'

Again he underlined his own distinction. This was a young man slick with the emphases. Trevor felt the invisible protection and afterglow of glorious love-making peeling away like the skin off of a ripe satsuma. There was

29

in Sergeant Hobson's blue eyes an echo of something he had read in Jill's *Guardian* about the nature of the zealot: he trebles the effort when he has forgotten the point. The article was about either Mussolini or Bugs Bunny, but the message was writ large in the Hobson face.

'A policeman?' asked Trevor, trying to fill the silence that was closing in around him.

'A graduate policeman with first class honours,' said Mr Wheeler, with the soft yearning of a headmaster who had spent long years trying to make too few names look a lot on an over-large honours board.

Mr Wheeler's praise bred a smirk on the sergeant's face, a smirk which Trevor rashly interpreted as a smile. He attempted a warming contribution to the conversation.

'That's jolly good. Mind you, I can't help thinking ... a university degree with first class honours ... seems a lot of trouble to go to, if it's a matter of vandalism. Lads been smashing things up again, have they?'

The lads of San Quentin High were accomplished and time-served vandals. Having some knowledge of what was waiting for them in so-called adult life, Trevor often felt inclined to sling a supplementary brick himself, in a gesture of solidarity and understanding, though this was not official education committee policy and contravened several byelaws.

'Not vandalism, Mr Chaplin. Not the lads, Mr Chaplin. Prowling, Mr Chaplin,' chimed the educated voice of Sergeant Hobson, like a bell-ringer, limbering up for the main event.

'Have the lads been prowling? Doesn't sound like their style.'

'I said not the lads, Mr Chaplin,' repeated Sergeant Hobson. This time the emphasis was unambiguously on the Chaplin.

30

Mr Wheeler stood up and walked to the door. 'I'm sure you'd prefer me to leave you in peace,' he said, and left the room without waiting for a judgement.

At that moment, Jill was moving into the finishing straight of her O-level dissertation on *Julius Caesar*.

'Now you might think that when Shakespeare whacked out this play, he was just giving the punters a few murders and battles about a load of boring old Romans. Well he wasn't. He was telling us what it's like to live in a police state.'

She glanced out of the window and saw the police car parked in the playground. She assumed the lads had been smashing things up again.

Sergeant Hobson was making no such assumption. He was accusing Trevor Chaplin of prowling in the immediate surroundings of St Luke's Church Hall plus the interior of the hall on the previous night. Trevor contemplated an insanity plea, then opted for the truth, though fearing it was the coward's way out.

'Yes. I was there. But I didn't prowl. I walked there. And I didn't prowl once I got there. I walked about.'

'You followed a young Cub,' said Sergeant Hobson. 'Why did you do that?'

'To see where he was going.'

'Do you often follow Cubs to see where they are going? Or was it a sudden impulse?'

Trevor, having dipped his toes in the truth, contemplated a nosedive into the whole and nothing but the truth, but feared that the keen-eyed young thief-catcher would be difficult to impress with tales of hedge trimmers and Bix Beiderbecke records. He tried a dash of righteous indignation: 'I'm not a pervert, you know. I'm dead normal. If you don't believe me, ask Mrs Swinburne.'

Hobson nodded sagely. He was something of a sage nodder.

'Yes, Mr Chaplin, we are aware of your Swinburne connection.'

'Pardon?'

Trevor assumed he was being rude. There were times talking with Jill when every word in the language became charged with erotic implication: wonderful sexy words and phrases like 'afterwards' and 'sea-shore' and 'man-sized Kleenex'.

The sergeant was not being rude. Sophisticated in deduction he might be, but in matters of applied erotica he was still at the starting-gate, sublimating furiously.

He handed Trevor one of the Swinburne election leaflets.

'You left that on the floor of the Church Hall last night.'

'Yes, I dropped them when I was kicked on the shin.'

'You were kicked on the shin?' Sergeant Hobson pounced on the admission. 'Why were you kicked on the shin?'

'I don't know. I was asking a civil question and –'

Hobson finished the story for him: 'You were kicked on the shin while the pack leader ran screaming from the building and telephoned us to report a prowler on the premises. We were there within minutes, found these leaflets on the floor, checked in our files, made the connection, Swinburne ... Chaplin ... and here I am.' He smiled, satisfied with a job well done and a community properly protected against footpads, malcontents and ne'er-do-wells.

The word 'files' disturbed Trevor. It jarred, as if Ella Fitzgerald had sung a wrong note in a Gershwin ballad. 'Am I in your files?'

The question delighted Sergeant Hobson. Ask any enthusiast to explain his hobby and inevitably there follows a passionate discourse on model railways, tropical orchids, the Indian mutiny constructed from used match-sticks or, in the sergeant's case, information.

'This is the age of confidential information about private citizens. Mrs Swinburne is in our computer because of her fringe political activities ...'

Trevor knew that Jill had a modest police record. She had been fined for sitting down in the road during an anti-nuclear demonstration.

'... and you are in our computer because you are a close associate of Mrs Swinburne. What was your civil question?'

'Pardon?'

Trevor remembered nothing about a civil question. Hobson did. He remembered everything about everything.

'You claim you were kicked on the shin because you asked a civil question. What was your civil question?'

'Ah!'

Now he remembered. He knew it would sound silly, but decided to plunge into his explanation, the way Dizzy Gillespie might soar into a trumpet solo, relying on providence to see him out at the other end.

'I wanted to know about Cubs football. I could tell you why I want to know about Cubs football but it might sound daft and in any case, I'm sure it's in your computer ...'

Trevor threw that in, midway between savage irony and a deferential creep. Hobson took it with total seriousness.

'I'm sure it is. What would you like to know about Cubs football?'

Stunned by Hobson's invitation, Trevor asked the first question that came into his head. 'When's the next match?'

'Tonight. St Matthew's versus St Mark's. Kick off seven o'clock, at the Alderman Wotsisname Memorial Playing Fields.'

Trevor was startled to be presented with the information he had been seeking so long and so painfully, from this unpromising source. He knew, theoretically, that the police existed to help people, but had never known it to work in practice.

Having come by the information, he decided his best plan was to run away and bury it. He looked at his watch, strictly as a ploy. The watch had stopped hours ago. He had forgotten to wind it the night before, in the ardour and heat of the immediate pre-duvet moment.

'I should really be teaching. I've got this big table-lamp project with Four B.'

'I have no reason to detain you further, Mr Chaplin.'

Sergeant Hobson's way of saying it implied he had at least five hundred reasons to detain him in solitary confinement for life, with no remission. Trevor was happy to postpone such discussions for a future occasion, and escaped into the corridor, with the brief exhilaration of one who has completed a dental appointment, knowing there are additional fillings still to come.

The canteen at San Quentin High had all the cosiness and intimacy of an aircraft hangar. Elsewhere in the school everybody talked and nobody listened. In the canteen, everybody shouted and nobody could hear. It was always called the canteen, despite Mr Wheeler's annual edict that it should be referred to as the dining hall.

Staff and students ate together, a calculated exercise in democracy and social conditioning. It was hoped that the young would learn decorum and fine manners from their teachers – like how to avoid skidding on a fallen fish-cake. In reality, all who entered found common cause and purpose: to cram the food in and get the hell out as quickly as possible, seeking peace and tranquillity in Walkman, wheelies, snogging or card-school.

Trevor Chaplin and Jill Swinburne sat in the midst of

the frantic, echoing turmoil, trying to have an intelligent debate. In its way, it was like many of the arguments taking place among the kids in the canteen, having at its heart the universal question: what shall we do tonight?

Jill had discovered that the local Film Theatre was showing *Some Like It Hot* with Jack Lemmon, Tony Curtis and Marilyn Monroe, and thought it would be a perfect if belated celebration of their second anniversary.

Trevor had discovered, from unimpeachable sources, that St Matthew's were playing St Mark's in a Cubs football match and while he conceded it would be a lousy way to celebrate their second anniversary, it might help solve the increasingly impenetrable mystery of the exploding hedge trimmer and misplaced Bix Beiderbecke records.

'I hate football!' yelled Jill, partly out of irritation, partly out of a desire to be heard above the clanking trays and voices, and reverberating cutlery, the tidal ebb and flow of gravy lashing against potato, custard against prune.

'You only hate football because –'

Jill finished the sentence for him.

'– because nobody's ever explained it to me properly.'

Mr Carter walked up to their table carrying a tray bearing the salad of the day and a glass of water. He had spotted their quarrel at fifty paces and fell upon it with relish.

'Do I observe corrosion in the afterglow?'

They both ignored him. He sat down, and sipped his glass of water, wincing at the taste.

'How do they manage to ruin water?'

'They have their methods,' said Jill.

'And why are you two quarrelling?'

Jill explained.

'I want to go to the pictures and he wants to go to a stinking rotten football match.'

Carter looked from one to the other, then lifted up his bandaged hand in a regal gesture.

'You should be doing neither. You should be solving the mystery of my hedge trimmer. The bandage may be smaller than yesterday, but the anguish is no less.'

Jill gave a Chaplin shrug, then snarled sweetly at Trevor: 'What time's the kick-off?'

'Seven o'clock.'

Then she took her revenge on Mr Carter, looking at his salad with alarmed innocence. 'Double-check your lettuce. I'm sure it just moved.'

Mr Carter pushed his plate of salad to one side, the fate of eighty-one per cent of meals served in the San Quentin High canteen on good days, rising to eighty-seven per cent on days involving fish or curry.

A sludgy-green Sahara, twice as old as time, punctuated with goalposts and rugby posts that had never heard of right-angles; that was the Alderman Wotsisname Memorial Playing Fields. Nobody could remember the late Alderman's name, and the plaque was covered with generations of graffiti. Scratch out 'Psycho Boot Boys' and you might discover 'Bay City Rollers Rule OK'. Scratch more deeply and you might well find 'Stanley Baldwin Go Home' or 'Kropotkin Lives'. These are ancient lands with primitive creatures waiting beyond the horizon to reclaim their birthright.

Trevor Chaplin and Jill Swinburne headed due south across the plain, in the direction of distant track-suited figures. At a range of half-a-mile, these figures clearly resembled an embryonic football match.

Their attention thus focussed, Trevor and Jill did not notice a man taking his dog for a walk, along an east-west axis. This man was called Harry and the dog's name was Jason.

*

Football has this in common with poetry, handwriting, love-making and post-Impressionist painting: it is an unrelenting revealer of character. The two Cubs football teams clustered on the touch-line were proof.

On the one hand, a dozen small boys, dressed as Sheffield Wednesday, were being harangued by an equally small man wearing an ill-fitting track suit. The small man was under the impression that the forthcoming game represented the last stand of Christendom against the infidel hordes.

'Don't give me any of this stuff about it's only a game! It isn't a game! It's football! It's a semi-final! I see any heads dropping, what will I have?'

The team replied in chorus: 'Our guts for garters!'

On the other hand, and at a safe distance, the opposing team, dressed in a faded replica of Brazil's World Cup colours, was being lulled into a more genteel moral purpose by a very large man in overalls and a flat cap. He was the size and texture of a Pennine hill and Trevor thought he had seen him before.

The large man's team talk was beguiling rather than fervent, owing more to Spencer Tracy than Henry the Fifth.

'It's only a game. Just enjoy yourselves, lads. All right?'

After the team talks, the large man and the small man approached each other, and started a wary conversation. It was clear to Trevor and Jill that some sort of crisis had arisen. They became aware of curious glances in their direction, followed by a careful approach to Trevor.

'I wonder whether you might be interested in reffing the game?' asked the large man.

Trevor smiled. It is always good to be seen as a Lone Ranger, moseying into town on cue for the emergency. The small man jumped in with the small print: 'No affiliations with either St Matthew's or St Mark's?'

'No.'

'And you know the rules of the game?'

Trevor was stung by the innuendo.

'I come from the North East, birthplace of the Charlton brothers, Jacky Milburn, Raich Carter ...'

'Howay the lads and whyebuggerman,' Jill added, by way of supplementary evidence.

The deal was struck. The small man presented Trevor with a whistle, a spare whistle, a stopwatch, a spare stopwatch, a notebook, a pencil, a spare pencil, a yellow card and a red card. He also told him to watch the opposing number six, because he was a killer.

Trevor walked to the centre of the field, breaking into a trot as the Geordie soccer heritage penetrated the soles of his Hush Puppies. On the touchline, Jill stood between the small man and the large man, cold and alienated in a man's world.

By the time referee Chaplin blew his whistle for the kick-off, the crowd had swollen to well over a dozen: parents, substitutes, passing strangers and the long-term unemployed with time to stand and stare. The first two minutes of the match were uneventful with twenty small boys chasing the lightweight plastic football in and around the swamp that had once been a meadow. It was in the third minute that the drama began.

The St Mark's centre-forward, a skilful nine-year-old with the poise and balance of a George Best, broke away with the ball and raced into the penalty area leaving defenders floundering and prone. He was confronted by the last bastion of St Matthew's: the goalkeeper, a ten-year-old with the poise and balance of Battersea Power Station. It was more in terror than malice that the goalkeeper tripped the centre-forward, but the rule-book pays little heed to

38

motivation. The boy had been felled and a penalty was his due. Martin Luther would have given a penalty, as would any Pope.

'Penalty!' screamed the small man on the touchline, seeing his star player rendered horizontal on the brink of triumph.

'Penalty!' agreed the large man, inwardly lamenting the limitations of his goalkeeper.

'Penalty!' cried the parents, substitutes, passing strangers and long-term unemployed, united by a need for drama in otherwise humdrum lives.

'Even I think it's a penalty!' said Jill, switching from her instinctive role of articulate minority.

The centre-forward and goalkeeper unmeshed and counted their limbs and they too agreed, amiably, that it was a penalty.

Only Trevor Chaplin was unaware of the nature and gravity of the situation. He was staring at the horizon, like a man who has caught a distant, tantalizing glimpse of a Holy Grail mixed with elements of a burning bush. In truth, what he had seen was a dazzlingly beautiful platinum blonde: to be precise, *the* dazzlingly beautiful platinum blonde, of the exploding hedge-trimmer and missing Beiderbecke records.

Penalty or no penalty, Trevor Chaplin had a far far better thing to do than he had ever done before. He placed his whistle and the assorted accessories on the ground and walked away in the direction of the blonde.

Sociologists have done little in-depth research into the relationship between soccer violence and referees who walk away in pursuit of a personal destiny. The semi-final between St Matthew's and St Mark's might be the only recorded example.

The violence was modest but passionate. The small man, puce with rage at the betrayal of his centre-forward, aimed an angry prod at the large man, who stretched out a gently restraining arm, which the small man mistook for a blow. A nearby spectator, father of the centre-forward, saw it as his civic duty to part the two men, who interpreted his public-spirited intervention as intrusion in a private dispute between nation-states. The entire crowd was involved in a mauling, shouting, confused heap when the police car arrived, blue light flashing and siren howling.

The only person not involved in the fracas was Jill Swinburne, lifelong pacifist and woman of initiative. She had walked smartly on to the pitch, picked up the referee's whistle where Trevor Chaplin had laid it to rest, and blown a sharp blast.

'Penalty!' she announced.

Two

Trevor Chaplin followed the dazzlingly beautiful platinum blonde at a distance of fifty yards or the metric equivalent along the winding streets of a 1930s corporation housing estate, a solemn and earnest environment, built too soon for precincts and too late for ginnels, offering brick boxes in rows with little gardens and wooden fences: all the essential ingredients of suburbia, but packaged in such a way that the inhabitants knew instinctively this was a place for common people, lacking the means or the will to become property-owners. Architects and planners send their messages and these are received and understood.

It was strange territory for Trevor. Still sensitive about the possible consequences of public surveillance, as a result of his experience with the Cub and later with Sergeant Hobson, BA, he was careful not to be too obvious in his trailing. He passionately wanted not to be noticed. The blonde hair and the swaying coat the shade of Picasso's blue period disappeared around a corner.

He did not know what lay around the corner: very much like life, he decided. He crossed a grass verge, circumnavigated what looked like alsatian droppings, and turned the corner.

The blonde had disappeared, not into thin air, but into a huge block of flats. Around the corner the mid-1930s, with its echoes of Al Bowly and Jeannette MacDonald, became the 1950s, era of the young Tommy Steele, and systems-built multi-storey living units. The front doors, painted in tasteful pastel colours chosen by highly-qualified experts in the town hall, opened on to balconies running along each of the ten layers of the pre-cast edifice.

Trevor calculated the odds. If he multiplied the number of balconies by the number of doors on each level, he would know how many times he would have to ring a bell, or batter his knuckles, prior to asking the inhabitant: 'Excuse me, does a dazzlingly beautiful platinum blonde live here?' Unless she answered the first door, in person, the likely results were alarming to contemplate.

At the Alderman Wotsisname Memorial Playing Fields, Jill Swinburne was also involved in an ongoing meanwhile situation. Having awarded the penalty to Sheffield Wednesday alias St Mark's, she became aware of the riot on the touchline and the arrival of the police, under the spirited leadership of Sergeant Hobson, BA. She waited until the spritely young centre-forward had scored the penalty, with a strength and panache beyond his years, then returned to the touchline, and the escalating fracas, with the proper zeal of a fully-paid-up member of the National Council for Civil Liberties.

Within minutes she was riding in a police car, driven by Sergeant Hobson, eyes shining with the glory of law and order triumphant. She sat in the back of the car between the large man and the small man, team managers of the two football teams. She was confused but not frightened. Hobson had made it clear that she was going to the police station as a voluntary witness to the events on the touchline, events initiated, in his view, by her two co-passengers. From the assorted yelling that had preceded their arrest, Jill had worked out that the large man was called Big Al, and the small man was called Little Norm. They seemed friendly.

Her main concern was Trevor. She had known him to walk away from many things in their time together – notably painful truths about himself. She had never known him to walk away from a football match. In the Chaplin world, that was a blasphemy.

Sandwiched between Big Al and Little Norm, Jill wondered what the Hell average-sized Trevor was up to.

Staring at the block of flats, Trevor was wondering very much along the same lines. He gradually became aware that he, in his turn, was being stared at, by a man with a dog. The man's name was Harry and the dog's name was Jason.

'Are you lost?' asked the man, a wrinkled refugee from a lost land midway between Batley and Samuel Beckett.

'Not lost ... more like looking for somebody.'

The wrinkled man, brimming over to cloth cap level with peasant curiosity, was eager to help.

'Who you looking for?'

Trevor hesitated. It was a good time to hesitate, because he knew it would sound silly. Then he said it: 'A woman. A beautiful platinum blonde.'

It sounded silly. The wrinkles on the man's face re-arranged themselves into a compromise between a leer and a smile.

'Aren't we all?'

'I think she lives in there somewhere,' said Trevor, ignoring what he took to be the joke, and pointing at the block of flats.

The man snorted and spat. 'Call that living?'

Trevor sensed they were on the brink of a two-hour monologue on the good old days, when people lived in back-to-back, verminous, grinding squalor but by God they were happy. He took several determined paces towards the block of flats.

'I might ask around the neighbours,' he said, more decisively than he was feeling.

'Neighbours!' erupted the wrinkled man. 'There's no such things as neighbours any more. That's why I have Jason.'

Trevor glanced at Jason over his shoulder. He was a small dog of no fixed breed, with a tail programmed permanently to the wag function. He would lick any belligerent neighbour into submission within seconds.

Jason was a nice dog, but Trevor Chaplin knew all about ageing Northern philosophers of the streets. They were people to walk away from, and quickly. He did so, in the direction of the flats. They were looming a little in the dusk, but he had been brought up in looming environments and he could cope.

The police station was a neat new building, designed with what public relations spokesmen call clean modern lines. It looked the sort of place where you might negotiate a decent mortgage or buy a fairly reliable micro-wave oven.

Sergeant Hobson stood by the entrance, waiting for his two suspects and key witness to proceed voluntarily into his hygienic, super-fresh nick.

Big Al made no move towards the police station. Instead he gazed across the nearby dual carriageway, towards the distant hills, like a Chekhovian heroine dreaming of Moscow.

'What's up?' asked Little Norm.

'I was just wondering whether to make a break for it,' said Big Al.

Sergeant Hobson shuffled as the large man continued with his musings.

'We'd probably get to the Mexican border before nightfall.'

'Are you lot coming?' snapped Hobson.

'Coming,' said Al, leading the others through the revolving glass doors. Jill Swinburne decided she liked this large man.

The off-beige door on the fifth floor opened as far as the safety chain would permit. A single eye peered through the slit.

'Does a dazzlingly beautiful platinum blonde live here, by any chance?' asked Trevor Chaplin.

The door slammed shut, just like the previous nine. Only the pastel colours varied. Trevor felt failure closing in on him, like mist across the marshes. He was also aware of the enormity of what he had done earlier: a Geordie, albeit living in exile, walking away from a football match. He made a decision, his second of the evening and well above his normal average. He would abandon the search for the blonde and return to the football match.

Jill sat between Big Al and Little Norm on a bench outside Sergeant Hobson's office. He had told them to wait there, so they were waiting there. It seemed to be Jill's fate to sit between these two men; where Al and Norm were gathered together, Jill Swinburne would be between them.

They had passed the time with formal introductions. It appeared that the men were known officially to the community as Big Al and Little Norm, but she expressed surprise when told that they were brothers.

Big Al smiled with gentle indulgence. 'We're often mistaken for strangers but we are, in fact, brothers.'

'I see. Well, my name's Jill Swinburne. I inherited the name from my ex-husband. Swinburne, that is. Jill was a present from my parents.'

45

'I've seen your name on an election leaflet,' said Big Al, with a sudden acceleration of interest. He was a man given to shifts into overdrive when ideas fired his curiosity.

Jill was delighted that one voter, at least, had read her election address.

'Jill Swinburne, your Conservation candidate,' she said, with proper pride.

Big Al pondered the implications of Jill's move into the public arena. A slow talker but a quick thinker, he unfurled his proposition in two stages.

'Tell me, Mrs Swinburne, what is the policy of the Conservation Party on police harassment?'

'We're against it. In fact, we're against practically everything.'

Big Al moved into stage two. 'You are the key witness to an alleged fight between me and Little Norm. Supposing I tell you that what you witnessed was not a fight, but good-natured banter between brothers ...?'

'About football,' added Norm. 'It's the only thing we fight about.'

'Except we weren't fighting,' emphasized Al.

Jill looked from one to the other, feeling like a Wimbledon umpire, and assessing the fine line between banter and battery, perception and perjury. She made up her mind without agony.

'I saw a friendly discussion between brothers.'

The men smiled.

'You just got yourself two more votes, petal,' said Al.

A sunset like a thin rasher of streaky bacon lay beneath menacing grey clouds, casting a last feeble gesture of daylight across the Alderman Wotsisname Memorial Playing Fields. There might have been ghosts and zombies lurking in the gloom, but there was certainly no trace of a football match. St Mark's and St Matthew's and their camp followers had departed. Trevor Chaplin looked this way and that, in search of a stray supporter or abandoned red card, but in vain.

Nor did he see Jason approaching, accompanied by his lugubrious owner, the raincoat still securely belted and the cloth cap firmly on the head as if welded, or fixed with a special screw thread, patent applied for.

'Still looking for things?'

Trevor pretended not to be startled, and threw in a shrug for additional protection.

'Not really. I was looking for a football match but ...'

He tried to walk away, but the word football had triggered a monologue, and there was no avoiding it.

'A football match? This is the place to look. See? There's the white lines and the goalposts and everything. Mind you, I did see a football match ...'

'Tonight?'

The man shook his head. 'February the fourteenth, 1953, that's the last time I saw a football match. Halifax Town versus Tottenham Hotspurs. That's when I resolved never to go again.'

The mathematical precision of the man's recall fascinated Trevor. This ancient dog-walker, despite his preoccupation with aspects of doom, also had the ability to stoppeth one in three at the drop of an eccentric fact.

Trevor accepted the bait. 'Why didn't you go again?'

'Too many people there. Couldn't see a bloody thing.'

Apparently this was the end of the saga about Halifax Town in 1953. Jason tugged respectfully on his lead, in the direction of a row of municipal saplings leaning with the prevailing wind on the northern boundary of the playing fields. The clouds were darker and the sunset had given up in despair. It was starting to rain.

'I think it's fairing up a bit,' said the man, with the acuteness of a pure-bred Yorkshireman.

'Yes,' replied Trevor, for the want of a more rational response to such a blatantly nutty observation.

Jason and the man, whose name was Harry though Trevor did not know this, meandered off in a northerly direction. It was obviously important to Harry that he should have the last word in any conversation and, rattled a little by Trevor's 'Yes', he tossed his one-line summary from a range of twenty feet.

'I'll leave you to pursue your desires and I'll pursue mine.'

When the rain falls on the hills and plains of the outer limits of Leeds, it is high, wide, handsome, resolute and vindictive. It rattled the window of the interview room where Jill Swinburne sat, face to face across a small square table, opposite Sergeant Hobson, BA. She was oddly relieved by the sound because it was the sort of room where a window comes as a pleasant surprise.

It was a room dedicated to the great god, Information. Hobson was hoping to elicit information from Jill Swinburne and so far was doing very badly. His first mistake had been to offer her a cigarette.

'No, thank you, I do not smoke and I'd prefer it if you didn't either. I am allergic to pollution.'

She used the special voice normally reserved to intimidate Three B, when they were getting stroppy about reading *Lord of the Flies*.

Hobson quickly closed the packet of Benson and Hedges, careful to leave the government health warning prominent. He smiled his odd little smile, a reluctant and occasional visitor to his quietly fanatical face.

'I very rarely indulge myself.'

'Oh, I indulge all the time, but I never smoke.'

The pride of the police force mentally rubbed out his approach to date and started again with a blank sheet of conversation.

'Mrs Swinburne . . . may we talk about the fight that took place this evening?'

Jill totally ignored the request, reached into her handbag, produced a notebook and ballpoint pen, purchased in aid of the Campaign for Nuclear Disarmament, and started to make notes. Hobson leaned forward.

'What are you doing, Mrs Swinburne?'

'I am keeping a verbatim record of this conversation, detective sergeant. At nine twenty-seven . . .'

She glanced at her watch. Hobson glanced at his watch. They agreed it was nine twenty-seven.

'. . . at nine twenty-seven, you *told* me that I had seen a fight, at a point in the conversation when I had given no indication that I had seen a fight.'

Hobson sniffed liberal-minded do-gooding in the air. He was right. Jill continued, confirming his fears: 'You are looking into the eyes of a paid-up member of the National Council for Civil Liberties, a subscriber to the *New Statesman*, and a prospective city councillor. You would be well advised to conduct this interview strictly in accordance with the law of the land.'

Hobson started a new page in his notebook. 'Tell me in your own words what happened this evening, Mrs Swinburne.'

Jill told him, calculatedly and at length, the story of her evening: how she had planned to go to the Film Theatre to see *Some Like It Hot*, throwing in the names of the leading players, director and screenwriter, and date of release, so that Hobson might have a complete picture: and how a teaching colleague from school had persuaded her to go to a football match instead.

'This teaching colleague ... would this be Trevor Chaplin?'

'Not only would be but was and is. Yes.'

Hobson relaxed a little. They had ploughed their way through cinema history and English grammar and hard evidence was looming. He resorted to the present tense for comfort.

'Good. You are at the football match with Mr Chaplin. What happens?'

'There was no referee. So Mr Chaplin refereed for a while, and then I refereed for a while. Then the police arrived. The rest you know.'

It was obvious that Hobson regarded this account as lacking both completeness and truth. He moved carefully in both directions.

'Are you telling me that at some point in time, Mr Chaplin stopped refereeing and you started?'

'Yes.'

'Why did he stop?'

'I don't know. He paused in the middle of the action, placed his whistle on the ground, and walked away.'

Hobson made a note in his book. As far as Jill could remember, walking away was neither a criminal nor a civil offence, but she would check on recent legislation once she returned home, assuming this man would allow her to return home. His immediate concern was to grapple, warily, with the heart of the matter.

'Mrs Swinburne, were you aware at any time of any disturbance off the field of play?'

'Yes.'

Once more Hobson saw a glimmer of hope, no bigger than a man's finger-nail clipping.

'Can you describe the disturbance?'

'Certainly. The police arrived, making a great deal of noise and fuss, spoiling a cheerful community event.'

Hobson's control slipped. 'Cheerful community event? We broke up a fight! Those two out there, they were hitting each other! There was blood!'

Jill shook her head, smiling with a tolerance that would have delighted Gandhi.

'I saw no blood. I saw good-natured banter between brothers.'

'Are they brothers?' Hobson was as startled by the news as Jill had been, an hour earlier.

'Big Al and Little Norman are brothers, though they are often mistaken for strangers.'

There was a silence, laden with mutual suspicion, as Jill closed her notebook and placed it, and the CND ballpoint pen, neatly in her bag.

'That is the end of my voluntary statement. May I go now?'

Detective Sergeant Hobson, BA, stifled a sigh as he saw immediate promotion drifting out of reach, but made no attempt to restrain Jill as she crossed to the door.

Outside in the lobby, Big Al and Little Norm were playing pocket chess.

'In the words of the Russian Grand Master, that's checkmate, sunbeam,' said Al, as Jill wandered over from Hobson's office. She read the game in a split second.

'No good trying the Bronte defence against a Priestley attack,' she commented.

'If it was football I'd thump him,' said Norm, as he packed the game away in its simulated plastic case.

'What news from the office of the ace sleuth?' asked Big Al.

'He might try to do you for GNB.'

'GNB?'

'Good-natured banter. Is there a public telephone in this place?' Jill was scanning the corridors and crannies of the waiting area. It was enough like a two-star hotel to offer the possibility of coin-boxes. Predictably, Big Al knew the answer.

'There's one down that corridor ...'

Jill took three steps down the corridor.

'... but it's been vandalized.'

All three of them were still laughing at this when Hobson emerged from his office to inform them, officially, that they could go home.

'Without a stain on my character, officer?' inquired Big Al.

Hobson did not reply. He seemed a little put out by the evening's events, and disappeared in the direction of the computer terminal, his best bet for immediate comfort and affection.

The pantiles, gnomes, wishing wells and minarets of the executive-pixie estate where Jill lived were lashed by gales and monsoon rains as she trudged towards the front door. Trevor's yellow van was parked outside. This would not help his case.

She entered the living room, dripping generously on to the carpet. Trevor lay on the settee, cuddling a copy of *Rothman's Football Annual*. He opened his eyes, and saw her gazing down at him, drenched and angry. They spoke together, perfectly synchronized: 'Where the Hell have you been?'

Trevor lost by several decibels, and suspected he would lose the row too. He had no idea what the impending row was about, but could see it coming, as inevitably as an avalanche droppeth on the place beneath.

He jumped up, eager to soothe. 'I'll make some tea, you change into some dry clothes and then –'

Jill finished the sentence. '– and then we'll have the row.'

'That seems fair,' said Trevor, moving smartly towards the kettle.

The row was preceded by tea and biscuits and a blow-by-blow account of their respective evenings.

Jill told of her voluntary trip to the police station, her meeting with Big Al and Little Norm and her interview with Hobson. Trevor listened, without interrupting, though the reappearance of the university-educated police-man in their life disturbed him.

Trevor had barely started his own edited highlights when Jill broke in: 'Why did you walk away from the football match?'

As Trevor edged into a mutter, Jill continued: 'Don't tell me – I expect you saw your dazzlingly beautiful platinum blonde on the horizon, and were wafted into another world.'

'Yes.'

This was not the answer Jill expected.

'Yes?'

'Sort of. I was reffing the match, and there was all that fuss about the penalty, and I suddenly saw her. And I thought: here's a chance to find out about the Beider-becke records and the hedge trimmer. So I followed her.'

'You must have found her.'

'No. The trail petered out at a block of flats.'

Jill was not amused.

Trevor protested, with all the unconvincing passion of the truly innocent: 'Honestly!'

She swung round her table lamp so that the light was directed hard into Trevor's eyes.

'Where were you at ten o'clock this evening, Mr Chaplin?'

'Here.'

'I telephoned at ten o'clock this evening, prepared to

grovel and beg for a lift home in the pouring rain, but there was no answer.'

'I was *nearly* here at ten o'clock this evening.'

Jill replaced the table lamp in its regular position, between the pile of back numbers of *Private Eye* and the chipped cut-glass vase, a wedding present from an aunt who, like the marriage, had since moved into oblivion.

'How could you be *nearly* here?'

'I was walking up the path and I heard the phone ringing. It had stopped by the time I was in the house.'

As he spoke, Trevor could see the precipice ahead. She was bound to ask him what he had been doing between seven o'clock and ten o'clock. She did.

'What were you doing between seven o'clock and ten o'clock?'

'I looked for the blonde at the block of flats, then I came back here. I called at the flat first.'

He tried to add the final remark as a casual aside, of no relevance to the immediate debate, or to the broader concerns of the human race; but Jill Swinburne could spot a significant throwaway as surely as Robin Hood could split a wand at a hundred paces.

'Why did you call at the flat?'

Trevor moved into his shrug-and-shuffle routine and took three more strides towards the precipice.

'You're going to think this is weird, but I met this bloke walking his dog. And he said he'd been to a football match in Halifax on February the fourteenth, 1953, and he couldn't see a thing because there were too many people there. Now, I couldn't believe there'd ever been such a situation in Halifax, so I called at the flat to collect this . . .' He held up the *Rothman's Football Annual*, as evidence of his good intentions and overall integrity.

Jill saw it as proof of terminal dementia. 'What is it?'

'It's a football annual.'

'Good God! Do they have annuals about it?'

'Yes. Once a year.'

'And did you find the statistics you were looking for?' asked Jill, drily.

'Yes. He was right. There were thirty-six thousand, eight hundred and eighty-five people there, which is remarkable, since, according to the book, the ground only holds twenty-five thousand.'

He held out the book, open at the relevant pages. Jill showed little interest in the information so freely and generously offered.

'You really are weird,' she said, with a quiet intensity that told Trevor it was next stop precipice.

'It only seems weird if . . .'

He never finished the sentence. Jill exploded at him.

'I was wandering the streets, in the pouring rain, trying to find a telephone that worked. When I eventually found one, you weren't here. You'd been prowling around a block of flats, looking for a blonde, after which you were farting about, checking some irrelevant facts about Huddersfield!'

'Halifax,' said Trevor, quickly. If he was having a bol-locking, it might as well be accurate. Jill ignored his factual footnote.

'So I stood in a bus queue in the pouring rain and the bus was full and most of the passengers were pissed and –'

For the first time in the two years of their relationship, Trevor yelled back at her.

'Well poor old you! Let's hear it from the gypsy violinist! Hell's teeth, you sound just like a wife!'

'How do you know? You've never had one!'

'I've listened to other people's. I got the message.'

Trevor stood up, to give his anger more space. He had thought of something that would really hurt, and he wanted to hurt.

'Call yourself independent and emancipated? You don't want a man. You want a taxi-driver!'

He looked around the room for his faded blue anorak. He usually hung it on the floor. Jill, startled by the truth and the venom of his remark, cooled a little.

'Where are you going?'

'I'm taking my football annual and I'm going home.'

The anorak was in a heap under the sideboard. Trevor put it on, stuffed the book into its pocket, and moved to the door. He looked back at Jill. The row was over and now they spoke quietly, like proper, mature, grown-up people.

'Pick you up in the morning? Usual time?'

'Yes, please.'

Trevor went home. In bed, he browsed for an hour among facts and figures about long-forgotten football matches. Jill, warm and alone beneath the duvet, read six chapters of a new novel from a pioneering feminist publisher. Trevor Chaplin and Jill Swinburne were content, for the moment.

At seven-thirty the next morning, at the neighbourhood police station, Detective Sergeant Hobson, BA, was hard at work at his desk. This was another item in a behaviour pattern that had caused his colleagues to reach a succinct conclusion about him: he was a loon.

In addition to arriving early and leaving late, he could make the computer work, a sure sign of eccentricity. Worst of all, he spent long hours in his room, talking to himself.

To be fair to Hobson – and it was no part of the local constabulary's philosophy to be fair to anybody, least of all a graduate copper – he was not talking to himself. He was speaking into a miniature tape recorder.

'Mary had a little lamb,' he said.

This was not a police-related topic, but a test piece. He

stopped the machine, rewound the tape and played it back. Through the ear-piece that he used for security reasons, he heard: 'Mary had a little lamb.'

Technology was in good order. Hobson could now proceed with his thoughts and reflections on law and order in the outer limits of Leeds.

'It is my view that the major challenge to the police force in the 1980s lies not with so-called major crime, but in the behaviour of people who, while outwardly respectable, show signs of social abnormality.'

He pressed the Pause button, while he paused to think about abnormality.

He reached a conclusion about abnormality, pressed the Record button, and spoke to his machine, saying: 'Out of every hundred people who behave in this way, perhaps one will eventually commit a serious crime. Our challenge ... *my* challenge ... is to prevent this. To this end, I am carrying out four in-depth investigations into the activities of selected individuals within the local community. The people I have chosen are subjects A, B, C and D.'

On Hobson's desk was a notebook, of a highly personal kind that would never be quoted as evidence in a court of law. He opened it at a page bearing the letters A, B, C and D. Alongside these were written the names Trevor Chaplin, Jill Swinburne, Big Al and Little Norm.

To his colleagues, Detective Sergeant Hobson, BA, was a lonely and solitary nut. To an objective outsider he might have seemed a bold crusader, waging war against the forces of darkness. The truth was somewhere in between. He was in the early stages of a PhD thesis.

As Hobson was rewinding and secreting his tapes, subjects A and B were getting out of subject A's yellow van, dragging themselves reluctantly into a new day of education at

San Quentin High. The previous night's row hung over them like low cloud with scattered showers. Jill carried the standard thirty-three exercise books, each containing a freshly–minted essay on the character of Jane Austen's Emma. Jill had hoped the kids would pronounce the young woman a bloody wet, but mostly they had toed the O-level line.

Trevor, unconcerned with the literary aspects of Jill's day, was eager to help with the weight.

'Can I carry those? I've got a couple of arms going free.'

'Save them for the next platinum blonde.'

He took this as an indication that the row was not yet over. He was on the brink of a token attempt at appeasement when he glanced towards the main entrance of the school and saw a familiar figure, topped by the equally familiar dazzlingly beautiful platinum blonde hair. For the second time in twenty-four hours, Trevor Chaplin walked away.

He did this smartly and discreetly, on the pretext of breaking up a small-scale protection racket in the playground. Consequently, Jill was alone when she was approached by the blonde who, at close quarters, was as dazzlingly beautiful as she had suspected.

'Mrs Swinburne?'

'I am she,' said Jill, pedantic and a little defensive for reasons she dared not analyze too closely. 'Who, with respect, are you?'

The blonde smiled, sending joy and an affirmation of life across all the land.

'Oh, everybody calls me Janey.'

Face, accent, demeanour and even, in an odd way, hair, combined to offer warmth to those around her and Jill's attitude softened in the glow.

'And what can I do for you, Janey?' she asked.

'You don't have to do anything. I've come with a mes-

58

sage from Big Al. He says thank you for getting him off the rap, and if he can be of any help to you in your election campaign, he's in his office most nights, until the sun goes down.'

Janey gave Jill a piece of paper with an address written on it. Jill looked at it without fully registering the information, then slipped it into her pocket.

'Until the sun goes down. Thank you.'

Inside the school an electronic whine indicated it was opening time for scholarship. Jill edged towards the door, trying her best not to spill exercise books.

'You'll have to excuse me. The siren is calling me.'

Then, as Janey moved away, a question landed in Jill's head.

'Is Big Al a friend of yours?'

She already knew the answer.

'He's my brother.'

An art teacher who had fled San Quentin with bruised aesthetics and a shredded ego after two terms had nonetheless left tangible signs of his stewardship over the three-dimensional and plastic arts. He had an obsession with primitive heads and the entrance hall looked like the annual conference of the national union of totem poles.

Papier mâché busts of all shapes, sizes, ethnic groupings and religious persuasions stood on shelves and in glass cases. Among them was a real head, attached to the body of Trevor Chaplin, where he stood in hiding. Jill found him without difficulty.

'You can come out now. She's gone.'

'Who?'

'Knock it off, smartarse,' said Jill. She expected him to shrug and he did. She threw him a comforting morsel: 'You're right. She is extremely blonde and extremely

59

beautiful. And I like her very much. Her name's Janey.'

'Janey?'

'Big Al's sister.'

'Your gangster friend?'

'Big Al is not a gangster and he is not my friend.'

Between the figures of an Aztec and an Ojibway Indian appeared a third presence: Mr Wheeler, the headmaster, academic gown spread in indignation. In such moods, according to Mr Carter, he looked like an Oxbridge flasher lacking the courage of his convictions.

'Mr Chaplin ... Mrs Swinburne ...' he proclaimed. He was given to proclamations, especially first thing in the morning. Trevor and Jill nodded acknowledgements that he had identified them correctly. He continued with his formal address: 'May I remind you that under the terms of the Education Act, school starts with a short religious observance and secular assembly ...'

Trevor generally referred to this institution as two swift choruses of 'Holy, Holy, Holy' and hands up who wrote shit on the gymnasium wall. For the moment he listened dutifully to his headmaster's perception of the gathering.

'The children are sitting in the hall. The members of staff are sitting in the hall. I am about to enter the hall, whereupon they will all rise. Your presence would be appreciated, to add completeness to the spiritual majesty of the occasion.'

'We were just ... preparing ourselves,' explained Trevor.

'Amen,' added Jill, as they walked into the hall.

The day's special in the school canteen was toad-in-the-hole.

'What makes it special is they use real toads,' said Mr Carter, as he sat down in the empty chair between Trevor

60

and Jill. The significance of the empty chair intrigued him.

'Are you two having a row?'

'No,' said Trevor.

'Yes,' said Jill.

'Very well,' said Mr Carter, 'I'll try an easier question. Did either of you see a dazzlingly beautiful platinum blonde hanging around the playground this morning?'

This time Trevor and Jill were in agreement; they had both seen the dbpb. Mr Carter moved to the next stage in his cross-examination.

'Who is she?'

'Her name's Janey and she's Big Al's sister,' said Jill.

'Who is Big Al?'

'I got him off a rap down the 87th precinct last night.'

Mr Carter prodded his meal reflectively: first the toad and then the hole. The hole was the more resistant to the touch. He decided to give up questions for the moment and resort to categorical statements.

'I don't understand who or what you are talking about. But I do hold that woman, and you, Mr Chaplin, personally responsible for my disability.'

He held up his hand, now wrapped in a smaller bandage than previously but still bearing signs of an unfriendly encounter with a recalcitrant hedge trimmer.

'Hang on to your disability,' suggested Jill. 'You might get a sticker for your car so you can park in special places.'

'I would prefer restitution, justice and compensation, in cash.'

'Tonight we might get all three,' said Jill.

Trevor stared at her. 'What are you talking about?'

'We're going to see Big Al.'

'When?'

'Before sundown.'

Mr Carter broke into their conversation, reluctant to be

61

left out. 'It's the only time to go. It gets so very crowded after sundown.'

'Mind you, I know how Mr Carter feels,' said Trevor as, later that evening, he drove his yellow van along unfamiliar streets in the outer limits of Leeds, according to directions given him by Jill.

'Something wrong with your hand?' asked Jill.

'No. All that stuff about Big Al and sundown.'

Jill explained the significance of Janey's visit to school that morning: how the big man wanted to help with her election campaign; how he had sent the slip of paper with his office address; and how, if Janey really was Al's sister, there should be a theoretical chance of resolving the mystery of the Beiderbecke records and perhaps even obtaining justice in the matter of Mr Carter's damaged hand.

But even Jill was startled out of rationality by where the address and the directions took them; she had not expected Big Al's office to be at the Tolpuddle Street allotments.

Tolpuddle Street had changed its name several times down the years, in response to changes in the local political balance. When the Tories were in office, it became Mafeking Street. When Labour gained control, it reverted to Tolpuddle Street. In recent times the warring factions had forsaken the matter, in pursuit of more pressing and creative challenges like making people redundant, and there was no money in the street sign budget. There had been a brief period when a myopic Liberal held the balance of power and somebody wrote to the local paper suggesting that since there was a hung council, Tyburn Street might be an appropriate name. The letter was ignored, and the issue had long since been consigned to the garbage chute of political dialectic. In any case, it was a modest little street; a lane with delusions of grandeur and the primary function of leading green-fingered artisans to the sanctity and seclusion of cabbage patch and rhubarb plantation.

The sloping path leading to the very heart of the allotments was too narrow and steep for Trevor's van, and they completed their journey on foot. They saw a neat, well maintained patch of fruit, vegetables and flowers, with a greenhouse and a shed. There was an air of friendliness and tranquillity about the place. Here, humanity could find peace, and listen to the beating heart of the good earth. D. H. Lawrence would have loved it, in his way.

Trevor and Jill approached the shed and tapped gently on the door. They did not see the man in the greenhouse.

'Can I be of any assistance?' asked Big Al, with robust politeness, emerging from the greenhouse clutching a tomato. Then he recognized Jill. 'Oh, it's you, flower! And you've brought the famous disappearing referee.'

'Your sister said you'd be available in your office, before sundown.'

'That's right, petal,' said Al, whose fondness for floral imagery was not quite the direct route to Jill's feminist heart, but she could tell his intentions were friendly.

Trevor looked at the greenhouse.

'Is that your office?'

Big Al shook his head, without dislodging the cap that was a permanent part of his approach to the world.

'No,' he said, 'that is a greenhouse.' He pointed to the shed. 'That is the office.'

It is conventional psychological wisdom that every individual requires an area of private space if a properly balanced soul is to be maintained in good order. The British working-class male has understood this for a century or more; hence the sheds and pigeon crees and chicken houses that proliferate throughout the older industrial areas.

Big Al's shed was tangible evidence of the theory and practice. It contained a workbench, three upturned boxes for sitting on, a kettle, a tap and, unexpectedly, a filing cabinet.

Trevor and Jill made themselves surprisingly comfortable on boxes that, in an earlier incarnation, had housed brown ale and processed cheese respectively, while Big Al made a cup of tea. He drew the water from a tap poking through the open window at the end of a pipe that snaked up the outside of the shed like a trailer for a John Wyndham novel.

'Pity you had to dash off last night, Trev,' said Al. 'We had this great fight on the touchline, me and little Norm, right good laugh it was. Good thing Mrs Swinburne came to the rescue with some perjury. That was a big help.'

He gave each of his visitors a mug of tea, first adding large quantities of damp sugar. Trevor expected Jill to protest. He knew sugar was deadly stuff for reasons to do with cholesterol or whales or the labour unions of Southern California; but for once Jill sat quietly, fascinated by this large man with the leaping logic and robust mind.

Big Al sat down.

'Now, in addition to helping Mrs Swinburne win a landslide victory at the election, I get the feeling there is some other way I can be of service.'

'You tell him,' said Jill to Trevor.

'Yes, you tell me, Trev.'

Trevor told him. 'Right. A few days ago, a young lady came to my door, selling from a mail order catalogue, in aid of the Cubs football team.'

'Janey, your sister,' added Jill, more to maintain her own grip on reality than to explain the story to Al, who moved in quickly with his own confident contribution.

'And the football team is St Matthew's. You saw them play last night. Grand set of lads. Can't play football, but

64

then, she's not my sister in the first place. Did you buy something?'

Trevor picked his way carefully through the story. He explained how he had ordered four Bix Beiderbecke long-players, only to receive an assortment of George Formby, Mozart, Everyday Spanish and cinema organs. He described Mr Carter's explosive adventures with the hedge trimmer. He left out the visit to Aristophanes Street and the pursuit of Janey to the block of flats. Like Jill, he could only cope with a finite amount of confusion.

Big Al listened to the tale with a mild frown of concentration, then stood up and crossed to the filing cabinet. He slid open the top drawer and took out a cardboard folder, running over with invoices and receipts. He selected a piece of paper, apparently at random.

'Yes, I can see what happened. It's a technical problem that crops up from time to time in the mail-order business. Little Norm cocked it up. Your friend Mr Carter ordered a Universal Executive Speedicut and we gave him an Okinawa Self-Assembly Supatrim. They're always blowing up. Same with the records. Wrong ones. It's a self-evident cock-up.'

'Is there any chance of uncocking it up?' asked Trevor, warily.

'Easy. No danger,' said Big Al, replacing the documents in the filing cabinet and pouring himself another mug of tea. 'We'll have it sorted well before sundown.'

Twenty yards from the shed was a belt of trees. Anybody wishing to observe a limited amount of the activity within the shed need only climb halfway up the third poplar from the left.

Halfway up the third poplar from the left was Detective Sergeant Hobson, BA, trying to clutch, simultaneously, his tape recorder, a pair of binoculars and a tree branch, his ultimate protection against the force of gravity.

After a brief recitation of the opening stanza of Jack and Jill, he then informed his tape recorder that he was maintaining a surveillance at the Tolpuddle Street allotments on subjects A, B and C. Pressing the Record button caused him to totter, but he did not fall. Hobson was not a man to fall easily or publicly.

Big Al finished his third mug of tea and then made his offer. 'Here's what I'm going to do, Trev. I'll take you down to my warehouse.'

'You've got a warehouse?'

'It's a warehouse like this is an office.'

'It's a shed?'

'No,' said Big Al.

'Subjects A, B and C left the shed at . . .' Hobson paused to check his watch and translate his reading into official police time: '. . . at twenty hundred hours.'

He decided eight o'clock was too neat and tidy, so rewound the tape and re-recorded the information, deducting three minutes to give his account greater professional authenticity.

'. . . at nineteen fifty-seven hours.'

He climbed down the tree, dropping his binoculars on the way. It was a straight choice between the denting of lenses and a simple fracture of the fibula and Hobson had the normal human prejudice in areas of self-preservation.

From the prickly sanctuary of a gooseberry bush he saw his three subjects climbing into the yellow van. He glanced back at the shed and saw Big Al's bicycle leaning against it. He concluded, with razor-keen perception that gave an inner glow, that Trevor would give Big Al a lift back to the allotments to retrieve his bicycle once their immediate assignation was completed.

He murmured to himself, without benefit of tape recorder: 'I know where they have been. I know where they will return to. I must find out where they are going.'

He released himself from a gooseberry thorn and raced to his car.

It was Big Al, curled up in the back of the van like a sack of potatoes, who realized they were being followed.

'We're being followed,' he said.

Jill turned round to check. 'It's the dreaded Sergeant Hobson.' She looked at Trevor. 'You'll have to shake him off.'

'You don't like car chases, you think they're silly. And besides, his car probably goes three times as fast as my van.'

Big Al made his pronouncement, massively, from the back of the van, like the voice of God, assuming Heaven to be centred on Hunslet or Batley.

'Here's what you do, Trev. Take the next on the left.'

'I knew there was an answer,' said Jill. 'Take the next on the left.'

The next turning on the left took the yellow van and, fifty yards distant, Hobson's police car, into a long straight road of the kind that crosses Australian outbacks, except this one was lined with one-time desirable semi-detached houses in the mid-stages of decay. The road had one additional property: a level-crossing inherited from the days when the railways brought prosperity to city-states and took day-trippers to the seaside. Few trains used this level-crossing, but it retained a nominal signal-box. Trevor, carrying out Big Al's orders, stopped by the level-crossing so that the large man could get out of the van and climb the rickety steps into the box. The van drove on, over the level crossing, towards a roundabout at the end of the road.

All this was observed by Hobson with a concentration that would have done credit to Einstein when he was trying to calculate what E equalled.

'Subjects A and B are driving along road in van. Subject C has alighted at level-crossing. Information timed at ... twenty thirteen hours. Just after ten past eight.'

Big Al's plan combined beauty, logic and efficiency. Trevor completed three slow circuits of the roundabout before turning back along the road, accelerating to the limits of the brave but clapped-out reconditioned engine. He stopped just beyond the level-crossing to pick up Big Al, at the precise moment that bells rang, lights flashed and the gates of the level-crossing closed, leaving Hobson's car isolated and alone on the wrong side.

The van drove off into the distance, a bright yellow taunt on the frustrated horizons of Sergeant Hobson, BA. He blasted a loud note on the horn. He yelled curses at the interior of the car: 'Shitbuggerfuck!'

Then, more calmly, and resuming his customary Oxbridge tones, he got out of the car and called up to the signal box: 'Excuse me!'

There was no immediate response, but eventually a slow-moving man emerged from the box. His name was Lol. So was his nature.

'What's up?'

'Where's the train?' demanded Hobson.

'Train?'

'This is a level-crossing. You closed the gates. There should be a train. Where is the train?'

Lol checked up and down the railway lines. He seemed genuinely perplexed by the lack of locomotion.

'Hang on,' he said, before returning to the confines of his box. A small traffic jam had built up behind Hobson's car

68

by the time Lol returned, smiling and clutching a large timetable.

'Sorry,' he said, 'clerical error. Could have sworn it was Monday. Daft really. But you can't help laughing, can you?'

Hobson restrained himself from laughter, climbed into his car and, as the crossing gates opened, stalled his engine.

In the yellow van, now a mile away and on its way to the warehouse, Jill asked the obvious question.

'Do you know the man in the signal box?'

'Yes,' said Big Al.

All three of them chorussed: 'He's my brother.'

Three

When Big Al promised a warehouse to Trevor and Jill, they had expected, give or take a brick or two, something that looked like a warehouse. The parish church of St Matthew, built in the nineteenth century in the black anthracite Gothic tradition, came as something of a surprise.

'This is the warehouse?' said Jill, as they approached the huge entrance doors, made from heart of oak with wrought iron hinges and a guaranteed creak.

'Yes,' said Big Al. 'It's a church really.'

Inside the church, Al led them down the aisle. Light filtered through the stained glass windows against a hanging mist that looked like incense but smelt like decay. In the high vaulted ceiling were the echoes of wedding marches, Sunday School anniversaries, passionate sermons and lost souls.

As they walked towards the altar, Al removed his cap. 'I'm no sort of Christian,' he explained. 'A fervent atheist, as a matter of fact. But St Matthew's has a Cubs football team and a broad-minded vicar. Reads *The Guardian* and goes on marches. And he always takes his hat off when he comes to our house so . . .'

He turned sharp left at the altar and headed towards a door nestling in the shadow of the pulpit. He unlocked the door. Trevor and Jill followed him down a narrow spiral staircase that reminded both of them of long-ago school trips to York Minster. They half-expected to meet a group of Americans coming up, pursuing a guide with a pretty umbrella.

At the foot of the spiral staircase was another locked door. They waited as Big Al unlocked it, pushed it open and switched on the basement lights.

They stepped into a department store. Electrical goods, gardening equipment, sharp suits and stereo miracles were lined up for inspection and consumption. Trevor and Jill stared.

A memory tugged at the back of Trevor's head. 'This reminds me of when I was a little lad and my mother used to take me to the big Co-op in South Shields.'

'Records in the corner, Trevor,' said Al, 'behind the tomb of the unknown vicar.'

Trevor made his way towards the corner in question, skirting a coffin-shaped plinth that might have concealed an average-sized cleric, his thoughts focussed on the musical rather than the spiritual. Even at this distance, he could see on the record racks names to make his spirit soar: Duke Ellington and Louis Armstrong, King Oliver and Fletcher Henderson, yes, and even the more esoteric among his idols, like Toshiko Akiyoshi and Wynton Marsalis. Let ancient clergymen lie in their well earned peace. Trevor Chaplin had found his heaven.

Jill Swinburne's curiosity was twitching in other directions. Normally the sight of a well stocked shelf of consumer items caused her to reach for the nearest copy of *Which* and embark on a fifteen minute monologue on aspects of the capitalist conspiracy; but this, she sensed, was something different.

'I know what you're thinking,' said Big Al, his cap now restored to its regular position, his face glowing with a thoroughly decent sense of pride.

'What am I thinking?'

'You're thinking, am I surrounded by stolen property?'

Jill denied such unworthy sentiments, though the idea had indeed flitted across her mind, without staying long enough to fester.

Al smiled. 'It's a natural assumption, bearing in mind where we are, buried deep beneath the house of God. You might well think this is all knocked off. But it isn't.'

'Coleman Hawkins!' yelled Trevor from his chapel in the corner, as he added another record to a small but growing pile. The other two ignored him.

'Some people would call this the black economy,' said Al, 'but we prefer to call it the white economy. We're trying to improve its image.'

He explained to Jill the history and background of his white economy. It had started eighteen months earlier, when the building industry, which he had served loyally as a carpenter and a joiner, declared him redundant.

He had moved through several stages. He had hung around street corners, he had hung around the library reading room, he had hung around betting shops, winning and losing vast sums of money in his imagination only, since coins of the realm no longer played any significant part in his everyday reality.

Then he and Little Norm had got off their backsides, initially by running the Cubs football teams of St Matthew's and St Mark's respectively.

'Is Little Norm a fervent atheist too?' asked Jill.

'No. He's a passionate don't-know, is Norm. He's like that with most things. Confused.'

Big Al was not confused. He had a certainty of under-standing and a sureness of touch in his business dealings that would have given him a seat in the highest boardrooms in the land, had not an accident of birth planted him in the outer limits of Leeds. Under his guidance, a simple door-to-door sales campaign in aid of the Cubs football teams had grown into a major community enterprise.

'We'll rewire your house for you, fit central heating, build you a bathroom extension. We've got stonemasons, piano tuners, poets, plumbers, aye, and a few teachers as well.'

'Roland Kirk!' cried Trevor, as his pile of records climbed a little closer to the barrel-vaulted ceiling, but nobody listened to him.

Al was eager to explain that he did not profit from the enterprise: any trading surplus was invested in football teams, old folk's treats and a minibus for unemployed school-leavers.

'It's a very clean economy. We deal in cash. We don't muck about with bills and invoices and tax and VAT. It's redundant, all that sort of thing.'

Jill was very impressed, and said so.

'So am I,' agreed Big Al. 'The vicar says we're like the Rochdale pioneers. We've re-invented the Co-op movement.'

'I *said* it was like the Co-op!' said Trevor, as he joined them, staggering a little beneath the weight of jazz music piled up on his eager arms, 'except you couldn't get Count Basie records in South Shields.'

Trevor Chaplin and Jill Swinburne were in a daze as they drove with Big Al back to the allotment where he had left his bicycle. Trevor was dazed by the prospect of listening to twenty-three long-playing records embracing every nuance of his beloved jazz from the Armstrong Hot Five of 1927 to the dazzling modernity of the Carla Bley band, an outfit which believed in saving time by playing at least three different tunes simultaneously. It would take Trevor a day and a night to listen to this music, and he was exhilarated by the prospect.

Jill was dazed by Big Al and the audacity of his vision. Ever since she had read *The Ragged-Trousered Philanthropists* in her second year at university, she had carried a dream in her heart of the self-supporting working-class community, of socialism with a smile on its face, of a happy land free of bureaucrats, grey men, repressive legislation and the sound of marching feet. Big Al had not created the happy land of her dream, but he seemed to be whispering of its possibility.

Big Al was not in the least dazed. He was curled up in the back of the van, quietly whistling a tune that might have been 'The Red Flag' or equally 'The Last Rose of Summer'. It was impossible to tell.

The yellow van arrived at the Tolpuddle Street allotments. The three of them climbed out, Trevor clutching his records, Al carrying the replacement hedge trimmer for Mr Carter. Contentment hung over them like the promise of a sunny day.

It was therefore a matter of profound sadness to discover that in their absence, Big Al's greenhouse had been reduced to a heap of crystalline rubble. Trevor and Jill were more outwardly shocked than the owner and principal victim of the outrage.

'That's a bit anti-social,' murmured Al, adjusting his cap two degrees to starboard.

'The rotten buggers!' said Trevor.

'Look on the bright side,' said Al, 'they haven't touched my bike. And whoever did it, you can be sure they've been conditioned by centuries of poverty and deprivation.'

He moved towards the shed. Apparently the subject of the wrecked greenhouse no longer interested him.

'We'll discuss it in the office.'

Before Al could unlock the door, they were diverted by the arrival on the scene of Sergeant Hobson, BA, who appeared from behind a tall plantation of sweet peas.

'Mr Chaplin ... Mrs Swinburne ...'

The big man jumped in quietly and firmly with his introduction. 'Al. Big Al. I'd shake hands but I'm carrying this hedge trimmer. Also, we've already met, at your police station.'

Hobson took a brief stroll around the wreckage of the greenhouse.

'Is this your allotment?'

'Technically speaking, no. I rent it from the Lord of the Manor. The Corporation, to be accurate. I'm just a humble peasant, tilling the land.'

'And this greenhouse. Any comments or reactions?'

Hobson clearly expected anger from Big Al, accusations of guilt, a great cry of rage at the fates that had caused such destruction. Instead, he was granted a shrug and a murmur.

'Well, as a greenhouse, it's knackered, isn't it? Somebody's smashed all the windows. That's a bit fundamental, whichever way you look at it.'

'And who might have done such a thing?'

'Somebody that doesn't like me. Or doesn't like greenhouses. Unless it's purely arbitrary, in which case somebody that doesn't like himself, or herself, or themselves, if there's more than one.'

Sergeant Hobson's evening had been dominated by failure and frustration. He had watched the allotment all evening, apart from a half-hour spell when he had tried to follow the trio on their errand to the warehouse. During his absence, a major act of violence had taken place. However he viewed his evening's work, it was not a major achievement in the annals of detection and law enforcement. This was his last chance to rescue a small victory from the catalogue of disaster. He tried shouting.

'For God's sake, you must have some idea who did this!'

The raised voice did not live easily with the well rounded

vowel sounds, the cleanly enunciated consonants, the comfortable music of Home Counties and minor public school. He just sounded silly.

Big Al's ponderous patience and understanding did nothing to reassure Hobson. 'All I'm saying is, inspector –'

'Sergeant.'

'Sergeant ... all I'm saying is, you'll get no reckless accusations out of me. I've indicated the culprit is probably somebody who is not at peace with himself. That must narrow it down a bit.'

'It narrows it down to practically the entire human race!' snapped Hobson, intending whiplash cynicism, but hearing it emerge as adolescent pique. He decided he would be better off talking to his tape recorder.

He walked briskly away through the allotments, almost falling over a trailing tendril of what looked like asparagus – could it be asparagus? He decided it probably could. In these God-forsaken acres of the United Kingdom, anything was possible, however bizarre. He could not blame God for forsaking the acres. He was a good judge, which, bearing in mind the nature of his job, was obviously why he was appointed in the first place.

The cosmic musings of Hobson's troubled mind were interrupted as he almost collided with a man and a dog, in that order. The man's name was Harry. The dog's name was Jason.

'Evening, constable,' said Harry.

'Sergeant,' said Hobson.

Harry glanced at the gathering gloom. 'Bit brighter now,' he said.

There was no gloom in the shed, where Al had lit an old-fashioned gas mantle. Like his water supply, the gas arrived along a pipe that trailed out of the shed via an open window.

76

Jill wanted to ask how, and on what financial basis if any, Al was connected to the major power sources in the area, but calculated the answer would be evasive to the point of invisibility.

Trevor and Al were negotiating a price for the jazz records.

'Let's see, Trev, that's twenty-three records of jazz music, plus the four you returned 'cos they were the wrong ones.'

'Minus the four I returned,' corrected Trevor.

'Plus or minus, it still comes to nineteen in my book. You owe us for nineteen records, say two quid a go, two nineteens are thirty-eight, less three quid for goodwill and a lift to the warehouse and back. Thirty-five quid suit you?'

Trevor was staggered. The going rate for an average long-player was a fiver at least, and he had paid twice as much for rare and exotic imports from Japan. Consequently, thirty-five pounds produced a broad smile and a smart movement of the right hand towards the wallet.

'No rush, Trev, we can put it on the slate.'

'My mother always said –' began Trevor.

Jill nipped in smartly. The sayings of Mrs Chaplin were, in her judgement, a better soporific than Horlicks. She preferred the sayings of Chairman Mao, in the original.

'On the way to or from the Co-op in South Shields?' she asked, hoping to deflect him from the turgid wisdom that threatened; but Trevor was determined.

'She always said, neither a borrower nor a lender be.'

'Good advice, that,' said Big Al, holding out his hand for the money. Trevor counted out thirty-four pounds, in notes and loose change. Then he turned to Jill.

'Can you lend us a quid?'

They left the office that was a shed, pausing briefly beside the wreckage that had been a greenhouse at the start of the evening.

'Do you really not know who did it?' asked Jill.

'Yes, I know who did it,' said Al, as he climbed on to his bicycle, 'somebody that doesn't like me. Good night.'

He rode off into the darkness, with a chirpy ring on his bell.

Driving home in the van, the burden of a hedge trimmer and twenty-three jazz records on Jill's knee reminded her of something she had almost forgotten.

'Mr Chaplin,' she said ominously. Even at their most intimate moments, the formality of the staffroom coloured their mode of address.

'Mrs Swinburne?'

'Before all this happened . . . the allotments, the ware-house, the greenhouse, Sergeant Hobson . . .'

'BA . . .' added Trevor.

'Before all this happened, we were having a row.'

'Gosh, yes, I'd forgotten,' said Trevor, with a smile, indicating he thought the row was a momentary wobble on their primrose path, now resolved. Jill's reaction indi-cated this was not the case. She reminded him of the source of the row: how she had travelled home from the police station on public transport in the pouring rain because he was checking some irrelevant statistics about Halifax Town, and perhaps in her view this implied a gulf in their cultural understanding that would be best satisfied by his moving out for a few days.

'If all you want is a chauffeur, maybe you should put a card in the post office window,' replied Trevor, who had been planning the reply overnight, in case the row came round again.

'In any case, it's going to be non-stop syncopated rhythm music for the next couple of weeks, isn't it?' she said, her knees buckling beneath the weight of the twenty-three records.

Trevor smiled and nodded. He was accustomed to her cavalier attitude towards jazz, and privately relished the idea of playing his new treasures in the comfort and familiar squalor of his attic. He sometimes played records at Jill's house, but music born in the bars and brothels of New Orleans did not sit happily in the semi-detached desirability of an executive estate.

They agreed, with a surprising element of mature understanding, that he should take his toothbrush and his records, return to his flat and pick her up in the morning at the usual time.

Jill enjoyed the experience of being alone. Having tried marriage, and abandoned it as an overrated institution, she had grown accustomed to her space. She welcomed Trevor's occasional visits, but breathed more easily when he was not there.

She slopped around her living room in slippers and housecoat, whistling along with a late-night symphony on Radio Three and idly failing to complete the *Guardian* quick crossword. She was stuck on 17 Across, the capital of one of the newer African states.

Funny, she reflected, how a devoted supporter of the Third World could be so ignorant about African capital cities, though on the other hand, she had no idea of the name of the Italian Prime Minister either, which maybe restored the balance.

Lulled by thoughts of this kind, and further comforted by the realization that she could manage very well indeed without a man in the house, the telephone call, when it came, did not frighten her, though it was clearly intended to.

The telephone rang, Jill answered it: 'Jill Swinburne.'
There was silence at the other end.

'Oh, come on, be a sport, at least give me a bit of heavy breathing.'

But there was nothing, so Jill hung up, made coffee and went to bed with Raymond Chandler.

Trevor had a silent phone message too. He was halfway through the second side of the first of his jazz records, a loud and riotous assembly led by the great drummer, Art Blakey. During the brief space between a couple of numbers, Trevor realized that the telephone was ringing. He switched down the volume on the record player and announced his name to the caller on the phone, then stood impatiently as the silent reply began and he could see the record revolving on the turntable and all that lovely music going to waste. Trevor Chaplin was not pleased.

'Oh, howay man, if it's one of you little buggers from Three B, at least have the courage to say so!'

Whoever it was said nothing, so Trevor hung up, and switched up the volume of the music louder than ever. The telephone call had not frightened him either.

Driving in to school next morning, Jill and Trevor agreed that the telephone calls had not frightened them. Trevor explained his theory that Three B were probably responsible but Jill thought that operating a telephone was certainly too complicated a technical operation for them. They had enough trouble with buttons and door handles.

In the staffroom, there was a short ceremony: the formal presentation to Mr Carter of his brand-new hedge trimmer, guaranteed not to explode and cause grievous bodily harm, or even trivial bodily harm. Mr Carter was touched, moved and puzzled.

'I'm overcome by the majesty of this occasion, but why are you here?'

Jill and Trevor stared.

'In the words of the great Spike Milligan . . . everybody's got to be somewhere,' said Jill.

Mr Wheeler walked into the staffroom and he too was puzzled when he saw Jill and Trevor.

'Mrs Swinburne? Mr Chaplin? Why are you here?'

'Everybody's got to be somewhere,' said Trevor.

Jill was catching a whiff of conspiracy, at a level way above the capabilities of Three B.

'Mr Wheeler, we teach at this school, day by day, week by week and year by year. Why should we not be here?'

'The telephone calls,' said Mr Wheeler. 'From your next-door neighbour, Mrs Swinburne, saying you had sprained your ankle and would not be at school today. And from your landlady, Mr Chaplin, saying you had sickness and diarrhoea, and would also be absent. I have reorganized both your timetables accordingly.'

It was difficult to tell what was the greater annoyance to the headmaster, the fact that he had reorganized the timetables or the unexpected appearance of Trevor and Jill and the consequent need to unreorganize the time-tables. He was not impressed by Jill's explanation.

'You will never have messages from my neighbours, Mr Wheeler, since they do not speak to me, and in any case my ankles are perfectly sound.'

'Exquisite,' commented Mr Carter.

Nor was Mr Wheeler impressed by Trevor's expla-nation.

'I haven't got a landlady, I've got a landlord and I think he's a limited company, because he calls himself And Co, and I never have diarrhoea.'

'I envy you,' commented Mr Carter.

Mr Wheeler arrived at a fairly obvious conclusion. 'I

assume this is some kind of elaborate practical joke. Some fool playing . . .' He hesitated, fumbling for a phrase.

'Silly buggers?' suggested Trevor.

'Tricks, Mr Chaplin, tricks!'

The headmaster turned sharply, with a Dracula twirl of his academic gown, and crossed to the door, muttering to himself about the waste of human resources involved in reorganizing a complicated timetable, only to have to rub it out and start again.

'And why,' he cried, as he reached the door, 'is it always you two?'

'Just a coincidence, I expect,' said Jill to the rapidly closing door.

As Jill and Trevor made their way to classroom and woodwork room respectively they agreed that the whole business was probably some fool playing silly buggers, and it would take more than that or late-night telephone calls to frighten them; but soon they *were* frightened.

Trevor Chaplin unlocked the door of the woodwork room and walked in to discover a noose dangling from a roof beam. It was a sturdy noose, made from good quality rope, the work, he decided, of a time-served professional in the noose trade.

Jill Swinburne, at the start of her first class of the morning, an O-level English group taking a preliminary stroll with Thomas Hardy, opened her desk and found, instead of her personal copy of beloved *Tess of the D'Urbervilles*, a dead cat. Jill screamed, very loudly.

There are no quiet corners in the canteen of San Quentin High, but Trevor and Jill set up invisible barriers against the surrounding mayhem as they sparred with their food and compared notes on fear. Trevor admitted he was startled by the noose in the woodwork room, without being as frightened as Jill had been by her dead cat. For a start, he pointed out, he had not screamed.

· 'I just climbed on the desk and took it down, and do you know why?'

Jill looked at him, worried by the smile twitching at the corner of his mouth.

'Why?'

'Because no noose is good noose.'

'Gordon Bennett!'

Trevor tried a modest chuckle. Jill remained serious.

'It is not funny, Mr Chaplin.'

'All I'm saying is, we've got to get it in perspective.'

'It's in perspective. I opened my desk and there was a dead cat.'

'You don't even like cats.'

'It isn't the cat aspect. It's the death aspect.'

Trevor attempted a rationalization of the morning's events. 'I wonder if they killed the cat specially, or just sort of picked it up somewhere?'

'You are joking too much, Mr Chaplin,' Jill responded. 'That's a sure sign that you are frightened.'

'Did Freud say that?'

'Yes.'

'Always knew he was a smartarse.' But Trevor agreed that he was frightened, too.

'How about a cuddle tonight?' asked Jill.

Trevor thought a cuddle sounded like a good solution.

'After school, you can collect your toothbrush and let's say about one of your twenty-three records.'

'Only one?'

'Yes. Only one.'

Trevor walked Jill back to her classroom after lunch, to act as an early warning system against unexpected items in her desk. He checked. There was nothing untoward.

'You're OK. Not a corpse in sight.'

'I don't find that funny. I don't find any of it funny.'

Trevor glanced down into the open drawer of the desk.

'I don't suppose it was a barrel of laughs for the cat either.'

Detective Sergeant Hobson, BA, had been warned on arrival that at an early stage in his career on the outer limits patch, he would be summoned for an interview with the Station Superintendent, Mr Forrest. The policemen around the station spoke of Forrest in tones that placed him in the hierarchy of power and persuasion partway between J. Edgar Hoover and Caligula.

Forrest sat behind a desk large enough for a decent game of five-a-side soccer. He was a man of equal height and width, without a trace of fat. He gave the impression that where other people had flesh, he had muscles, and where other people had muscles, he had pre-stressed concrete. His accent was Liverpool-Irish, with a bloodshot quality.

'Thought it was time I took a closer look at our token graduate policeman.'

There was a Celtic cadence to the word policeman, and a gently venomous emphasis on the word token. Forrest got up and walked around the desk to take the promised closer look. He was like a dealer inspecting a second-hand car of doubtful origin. The inspection completed, he wandered across to a cabinet where stood a coffee pot and cups. He poured himself a cup, then, to Hobson's surprise, added ice and a splash of soda. Hobson concluded it was not coffee in the coffee pot.

Relishing the elastic silence, Forrest returned to his desk and picked up a file. He opened it.

'I have been reading your reports, Hobson. I see you spent the whole of last evening at the Tolpuddle Street allotments. Why?'

It was a rumbling sentence, ending in a bark with a touch of snarl.

'Not quite the whole of last evening, sir,' said Hobson.

'But the greater part. Are you planning to nick some broad beans for loitering? Or is somebody contemplating gross indecency with a bunch of dahlias?'

'I had good reason for keeping a surveillance at the allotments, sir.'

A graduate policeman with first class honours should have realized that Forrest was a man who had been chewing up and spitting out good reasons for the greater part of his professional career.

'You had good reason? And did anything happen to justify your good reason?'

'Some damage was done to a greenhouse.'

'How much damage?'

'It was destroyed, sir.'

Forrest smirked with the satisfaction of a man who has read the report and already knows how the story ends.

'Who destroyed it, Hobson?'

There was a pause of the kind developed and, who knows, patented by Harold Pinter.

'I wasn't actually there when it happened, sir.'

'Let me clarify this in my mind, Hobson. You spend the greater part of the evening at the allotments because you have good reason to think that something nefarious might take place. You slip away for a few minutes and while you are away, the nefarious deed comes to pass. Is that a fair summary?'

'An accurate summary,' said Hobson, 'but not entirely fair. If I may be permitted to explain –'

Forrest did not permit Hobson to explain. 'I don't want explanations. I want people nicked. I want villains put away for life. I want punishment and retribution. The old-fashioned virtues.'

He topped up his coffee cup before changing tack.

'I am also told, Hobson, that you spend long hours in your room, talking to yourself.'

'I dictate my reports and observations into a tape recorder, sir, in a quest for greater efficiency.'

'And you sit in front of the computer for days on end.'

Forrest hated computers almost as much as good reasons and eager graduate policemen with ambition in their fresh faces.

'I make full use of the technology that is now available to the police force, sir.'

'You make full use of the fact you're the only bugger that can make it work.'

'That is scarcely my fault, sir.'

A touch of irritation crept into Hobson's voice. The word 'sir', enunciated with respect and deference at the start of the interview, now carried an edge of contempt. It was another mistake. Forrest had never seen a play in his life, but could spot a subtext across a crowded billiard hall.

'And you use poncey words like scarcely.'

Forrest stood up. He paced around Hobson in slow circles, like a hungry dog circling a bone, assessing its potential.

'You're a graduate copper with a good degree. Nothing wrong with that. I hold up my hand in favour of educated policemen. In principle. In practice, you're all a pain in the arse.'

His colleagues had warned Hobson that the interview would culminate in a soliloquy from Forrest about his younger days, on the beat in Liverpool. Hobson wondered whether middle-aged police officers walked down memory lane in twos. He decided to postpone speculation and listen.

'I learned my policing on the beat in Liverpool. The hard way. Reassembling bits of sailors and dockers on a

86

Saturday night. Preventing Armageddon between husbands and wives, Catholics and Protestants, harlots and protectors. Persuading murderers and gangsters and bank robbers to move to Manchester. Whereas you ...'

The soliloquy was over. Now it was purely personal.

'... you spend your time talking to yourself. Playing with buttons on a computer. Hanging around allotments watching the grass grow.'

'I do have good reasons for my actions, sir.'

'Try me with one.'

Hobson took a nose-dive into the deep end of reason.

'I am working on a thesis, sir.'

Forrest guffawed, the first time he had laughed since Hobson walked into the office. It was a sight and sound more sinister than his mumbling and snarling.

'Now, Hobson, you think you've got me there. You think I don't know what a thesis is. Well I do. I've got a daughter at a polytechnic and she's doing one. Great fat bundle of words about sod all. What's yours about?'

'The grey areas on the fringe of normal crime. The investigation, in depth, of apparently normal individuals whose behaviour is in some measure unusual, eccentric, subversive or bizarre.'

'Bent?'

'In a sense, yes, sir.'

'And what happens to this thesis when it's finished?'

'I hope to get my PhD.'

Forrest nodded. He was spotting another subtext. 'Not content with being a graduate copper, you want to be a supergraduate copper?'

Hobson nodded in his turn, and even attempted a modest smile, though the majority of the human race would have reckoned it a smirk.

'I am not without ambition, sir.'

Forrest had read the subtext accurately. The young man

87

was a zealot. Given a decent incentive, he would march into Poland across broken glass. His obvious limitations were that he read books, spoke much too prettily and had only bum-fluff on his chin. The lad was ambitious, but would not be dangerously so for several years, by which time they would probably give him a college to run.

The superintendent summarized his feelings.

'Well, on the one hand, your thesis sounds like a total waste of time for everybody concerned. On the other hand, it will serve the useful purpose of keeping you out of the way while the rest of us get on with some proper, grown-up thief catching. Right. Sling your hook.'

Hobson did not immediately realize that this was Forrestese for kindly leave my office. The subsequent silence convinced him. He made his way to the door, opened it, and was about to depart when Forrest called to him.

'One more thing. A little bird tells me you're trying to nick Big Al. Don't waste your time. You'll wind up as barmy as he is.'

'Thank you, sir. Noted.'

Outside in the corridor, Hobson wondered about the last-minute reference to Big Al. He had a feeling that it was his turn to glimpse a subtext, fleeting, tantalizing and momentarily out of reach.

Thoughts of nooses and dead cats evaporated from the Swinburne living-room during the course of the evening. By ten o'clock, Trevor and Jill were halfway through the second bottle of Frascati, and they were sitting together on the settee, enjoying the peace of no music, the silence of no television, the sharing of simple and silly talk.

'You can't beat it,' said Trevor. 'An old-fashioned evening, sitting around the gas-fired central heating.'

'Just like the days when you ran barefoot down the cobble-stone streets of Tyneside.'

'Throwing bricks at the lamplighter and singing traditional Geordie songs like "The Lost Chord" and "I Want To Be Bobby's Girl".'

They enjoyed an honest-to-goodness, unpremeditated, plonking kiss. Then Trevor topped up the wine in their glasses. Neither of them spoke about it, but they were relieved that the evening had been free of mysterious phone calls and variations on the dead cat theme. Perhaps it was the relief that caused Trevor to lurch into a discussion about their relationship; normally it was Jill who took initiatives in matters of intimate emotion.

'I think we should talk about us,' he said.

'What about us?'

'I don't understand us. Twenty-four hours ago we were having a row about Halifax Town, and I cleared off with my records and toothbrush for a trial separation. Now we're together again. The same us. Nothing's changed. Except we're not really rowing any longer. We're . . . sort of happy. Aren't we?'

He realized happy was a reckless word to fling into the conversation even during the second bottle of wine, but Jill was amenable.

'Yes, we're happy.'

'Why?'

'Because we came home just a little bit frightened, and people always grow closer when they're a little bit frightened. Most marriages survive on that basis. Because people are scared of the alternative.'

Trevor, anxious to hang on to the happiness a little while longer, kissed her again, then asked: 'Is fear the only reason people stay together?'

'Of course not. Sometimes they have lots of things in common.'

'What sort of things?'

'Making raffia mats. The Labour Party. Heavy drinking. Golf.'

Trevor shook his head with unusual vehemence. 'No. Things in common doesn't work.'

Jill guessed, with her usual acumen, that Trevor was on the verge of a great confession; the only question was whether he could be persuaded to own up.

'Tell me.'

'What?'

'Give with the great confession, Mr Chaplin. I know it's there. Share it with the world. You know it makes sense.'

He topped up his wine glass. 'Can't do it without artificial aids.'

'I take it you're talking about great confessions?'

'Listen, Mrs Swinburne. What I have to tell you is this. I was once engaged.'

He stopped. That was apparently the end of the statement. Jill gawped at him.

'Is that it?'

'Yes.'

'Oh come on. Let's have some gory details. Sexual abnormalities. Spot of homely fun. Father's horse-whip.'

Trevor shook his head. 'There wasn't anything like that.'

'OK. So tell me the girl's name.'

'Helen.'

'Of Troy?'

'Of Tadcaster.'

'Helen of Tadcaster.'

Jill raised her glass and drank a toast to Helen of Tadcaster, the woman who had once passed through Trevor Chaplin's life, and then leaned closer to him, eager for more details.

'Tell me more, and I might be generous with my favours at duvet time.'

Trevor told her more, though his knowledge of Frascati's track record in the duvet stakes made him confident of eventual favours, with or without intimate confessions.

'Helen. From Tadcaster. Met her at a jazz club. Went out with her. Went on a day trip to London, so we could go to Ronnie Scott's. Got engaged. Ordered the ham salads. Made a list of presents. Selected a best man. Then she gave me the elbow.'

'My God! You don't mean dot dot dot she jilted you?' said Jill, with a sudden attack of amateur dramatics brought on by the wine, and placing a consoling hand on his left thigh.

Trevor nodded: 'She said I was boring. No surprises. We agreed about everything. That's what I mean. Things in common doesn't work. I mean, look at us two ...'

'Yes?'

The hand on his thigh moved a couple of inches in a highly significant direction.

'We disagree about everything. Politics, jazz, football, newspapers, curtains, food. We have rows all the time. Me and Helen had boredom all the time. You can't win. No wonder I'm frightened of women.'

Jill's hand paused on its journey along the centre-lane of the corduroys. This was a really intimate confession that needed talking through thoroughly.

'You're frightened of women?'

'Isn't everybody? Apart from women?'

'But you're brave for admitting it.'

The lines on Trevor's forehead crinkled a little as he tried to concentrate, which was not easy in the context of a hand on the thigh, deep personal revelations and an unusual amount of traffic noise from outside. He plunged in: 'Does that mean, if I tell you I'm also terrified of dentists and doctors and banks and envelopes with windows and spiders and slugs and some dogs, notably alsatians ... am I really brave to be frightened of all those things?'

'You're brave for admitting it. Though generally speaking you're a spineless coward.'

The smile took the cutting edge from the insult. Hands and arms regrouped and they embraced.

'You still make the bells ring for me, sweetheart,' said Jill as she became aware of bells ringing somewhere around the parish. They broke away and switched their thoughts from a prospect of duvets to the reality of bells. It sounded as if a fire engine was driving up the path.

'Are you on fire?' asked Trevor.

'Don't be personal.'

Above the sound of the firebell, there was an additional descant of a police siren, and the urgent shouting of men in search of a crisis. Lights were flashing in the street outside.

Jill got up from the settee and crossed to the window. She saw a fire engine and police cars, and uniformed figures rushing purposefully in many directions. As if bells enough were not ringing, the telephone joined in, at the same time as somebody knocked on the front door, seemingly with a large axe.

'You answer the door, I'll answer the phone,' said Jill.

It was their turn to dash in many directions. It took Trevor and Jill five minutes to realize they were in the midst of a false alarm, and half-an-hour to convince the fire brigade and police. The firemen had a natural, professional inclination to want to remove the roof, as a precautionary measure, but were persuaded otherwise by offers of hot tea.

An hour later, Trevor and Jill sat on the settee, failing to recapture the Frascati-flavoured tenderness of mid-evening, and grappling with the logic that had brought the emergency services, in strength, to sully their gentle love-play.

'That feller that knocked at the door with his axe,' said Trevor, 'he wanted to know about the explosion.'

'Explosion? That's funny.'

'I don't think explosions are funny, even when they never happen.'

'While you were at the door, I was answering the telephone, remember? And the voice on the phone said: "Sorry about the fuss, it was all a mistake, the explosion's tomorrow night."'

Trevor Chaplin and Jill Swinburne were frightened again.

Whenever the day dawned bright, sunny and optimistic, Harry took his dog, Jason, for a long walk. He did the same if the day dawned bleak, wet and laden with doom.

Their walks observed a meandering discipline. There were fixed points on the route, according to the day of the week, but built around a framework of pubs, betting shops, football pitches, barbers shops and street corners where the long-term unemployed gathered to smoke, spit and reflect on their rotten lot.

Harry and Jason always crossed main roads at the proper places, when the little man on the traffic lights shone green. It was a key part of any civilized dog's education. This morning, as they crossed the High Street, crammed to the brim with rush-hour commuters, the vehicle at the head of the queue was a yellow van.

'I know him,' said Trevor.

'Who?'

'The bloke with the dog. His name's Jason.'

'What's the man called?'

The lights changed, and the yellow van pulled away in the direction of San Quentin High.

Harry and Jason walked on. There was in Harry's stride an unusual sense of purpose and direction. He knew where he was going and Jason was content to follow. By way of a shopping precinct full of abandoned launderettes and takeaways, past a locked-up adventure playground and through the only surviving ginnel in the area, they made their way to the police station.

At the desk in the entrance lobby, he announced his purpose to the duty officer, a sleepy-eyed constable whose thoughts were directed towards that afternoon's card at Newmarket.

'Officer,' said Harry, 'I have come to offer my services as an informer. No, more than that. As a supergrass.'

The officer immediately filed Harry under L for Loony and observed the precinct's new standard procedure in such cases. He sent him along to Sergeant Hobson's office.

'A supergrass?' said Hobson, who had read about the breed in national newspapers, and seen documentary programmes about them on BBC2, but had never met one face to face.

'I want to play my part in cleansing society of all evil,' announced Harry, as Jason scratched himself, before lying down for a sleep.

Hobson opened his notebook and unscrewed the top from his fountain-pen, a leaving present from colleagues at his previous workplace. It was not an expensive pen, because they were quite pleased to see him go.

'Perhaps you could give me some details.'

Harry and Jason scratched and shuffled in counterpoint, prior to his announcement.

'They have made of my father's house an house of merchandise.'

Harry sat back in his chair with a look that implied:

pick the bones out of that. But Sergeant Hobson was an educated man, and not to be outquoted by an itinerant Northern dogwalker, especially one who had annoyed and embarrassed him during his surveillance at the allotments.

'Very well. Who, in this case, are the changers of money and the sellers of oxen and sheep and doves?'

'Big Al.'

Hobson's knowledge of the authorized version had taken Harry by surprise, and the name shot out as an automatic response, clearly against his better judgement. Hobson wrote 'Big Al' in his notebook.

'Mind you,' continued Harry, covering his tracks, 'I'm not saying it's him, as such. And it's certainly not oxen and sheep and doves. It's more your electrical goods and gardening tools and deckchairs and stuff.'

Hobson nodded, trying to look sagely wise and twenty years older than the age on his birth certificate. Superintendent Forrest would have been at the bottom of the case in twenty seconds flat, including the count, and he briefly wished he had spent his salad days on the beat in Liverpool. But he was stuck with intimidation through posh accent and superior education.

'Translating what you say into modern English, you seem to be telling me that Big Al is operating some kind of racket from a church. Would that be a correct assumption?'

'You must make a scourge of small cords and drive him from the temple. You must overthrow the tables of the money changers.'

It was like a dress rehearsal for a revival meeting. Hobson raised a hand, palm outwards, suggesting silence. He had a genuine fear that Harry would recite the entire Gospel according to St John, and his notebook could not cope, nor was it admissible evidence in any case.

'Just give me the facts about Big Al and the church.'

'How much are you going to pay me?'

This was the moment Hobson had feared and he hid quickly behind righteous indignation.

'Pay you? In all my years in the police force I have never paid for information!'

'Suit yourself,' said Harry, who got up, disentangled Jason's lead from the table leg and walked slowly to the door.

'Five pounds.'

Harry and Jason returned to the negotiating table.

Mr Carter, carrying his tray of curried indefineable and rice, found Jill Swinburne sitting on her own in the school dining hall. He sat beside her, uninvited.

'Where is the smiling Adonis of the woodwork room today?'

'Mr Chaplin is not here. He is somewhere else.'

'Thank you, Mrs Swinburne.'

It was a long-standing tradition of their relationship that Jill gave unhelpful or confusing answers to Mr Carter's questions. They both enjoyed the game and it took their minds away from tiresome matters like education and canteen food.

On this occasion, Jill had not lied. Trevor was somewhere else. He was at the house, checking for explosives. It had seemed a sensible plan when they first discussed it. A man had telephoned the previous night, warning them that the real explosion was yet to come. The obvious response was to check the house at regular intervals through the day for signs of an impending explosion.

Trevor Chaplin did not know what signs of an impending explosion looked like. He searched all around the house and garden. He found a note from the milkman saying he would call for his money on Saturday. He found some fish-and-chip wrappers, deposited by a late-night boozer. He found a rusty trowel. He found no signs of an impending explosion.

Mr Carter had abandoned his curry in the hope of prolonging his life sufficiently to reap the benefit of superannuation, while Jill sipped warily at a glass of water. She decided it was her turn to ask a silly question.

'Are you doing anything tonight, Mr Carter?'

'My loins throb to hear such a question, Mrs Swinburne.'

Jill shook her head, indicating he had driven into a No-Entry zone, and handed him a leaflet.

The leaflet announced, in a mixture of upper and lower case, that Your Conservation Candidate, JILL SWINBURNE, was to address a meeting of the voters that evening in Room 17A of the Adult Education Institute.

Mr Carter absorbed the information with controlled rapture. 'In principle, I would love to support your brave and gallant cause, my dear, but there's a probing documentary on Channel 4, involving glimpses of nudity, that I am planning to sleep through.'

But Jill Swinburne was not listening. She was looking at the handbill for her election meeting at the Adult Education Institute and speculating whether her house might be the wrong place to check for signs of an impending explosion.

Sergeant Hobson fully expected an explosion when he asked Superintendent Forrest for permission to carry out a raid on St Matthew's church. He got one.

'Listen, son, I'll tell you about raids. You can raid anything. A casino, a house of ill repute, you name it. A pound to a penny it belongs to a member of parliament or a merchant banker. But a church? You're into archbishops, and after that, plagues of frogs and locusts, the murder of the first-born.'

Hobson battled on gamely: 'Sir, I have reason to believe the church contains stolen property and I could nail a major crime syndicate, bang to rights.'

The slang did not fall happily from his lips. It was like George Formby singing Tosca, or Raphael scribbling rude graffiti on a chapel wall. Curiously enough, it convinced Forrest of Hobson's sincerity of purpose.

'I'll do a deal with you, son. You ask for volunteers and I'll look the other way. If it's a cock-up, officially it never happened. You might be in shtuck but I won't.'

'And if it's a success?'

'I shall claim full responsibility,' smiled Forrest.

'Is that entirely fair?' frowned Hobson.

'Of course not. That's how I come to have a high rank and a big flash office, while you're pissing about with frogs and locusts.'

Tingling with the injustice of the hierarchical system, Hobson departed in search of volunteers. He had one source of satisfaction; he had not mentioned Big Al, and Forrest had not asked about him.

Only two volunteers were forthcoming for the proposed raid, the semi-legendary Joe and Ben. These were two ageing detective constables who resolutely refused to take any initiative that would bring them promotion, while at the same time perfecting a double act based, in their view, on a gritty Northern version of Starsky and Hutch, though in the opinion of their colleagues they were closer to Laurel and Hardy.

They had caught a sniff of overtime in Hobson's invitation and wandered into his room twenty minutes after the agreed hour for the briefing. Hobson had drawn a plan of the church and the surrounding streets on a large blackboard.

'Fabulous drawing, sergeant,' said Ben.

'Which cinema is it?' asked Joe, lighting a cigarette.

'This is a plan of St Matthew's Church, and I would rather you didn't smoke during this briefing.'

'All right if we steam a little?' asked Ben.

The Adult Education Institute was built in the nineteenth century by a paternalistic mill-owner with the stated aim of bringing spiritual uplift to the artisans of the area. A hundred years later, it still had not succeeded. The building, designed in the Gothic Inspirational manner, was now a hive of small rooms in which groups of predominantly earnest people discussed D. H. Lawrence, watched *The Battleship Potemkin* or threw pots. It was not unusual for six people to be plotting revolution in Room 5, while across the corridor in Room 6, another six people were plotting counter-revolution. All twelve would meet in The Five Bells afterwards for a pint.

Jill's meeting was to start at seven-thirty pm. She and Trevor arrived an hour early, to check the premises in general, and Room 17A in particular, for signs of an impending explosion. They found none. The room had seating accommodation for a hundred people. Trevor sat in one of the fifth generation Bauhaus stacking chairs while Jill put campaign leaflets on the other ninety-nine.

By seven o'clock, the audience consisted of Trevor Chaplin, but there was still half an hour to go, and traditionally the local electorate was sluggish but loyal.

At seven o'clock Hobson sat with Ben and Joe in his car, parked in an alley commanding a clear view of the parish church of St Matthew. They had been there since six-fifteeen or what Hobson insisted on calling: 18.15.

Joe and Ben were playing the twenty-fifth round of a game.

'I spy with my little eye something beginning with C.'

'Church.'

'Right. Your turn, Ben.'

'I spy with my little eye something beginning with C.'

'Church.'

'Right. Your turn –'

'Oh do be quiet!' said Hobson, with a subdued shriek.

'Sorry, sarge,' said Ben, 'but you must understand, we're missing a probing documentary on Channel Four, with glimpses of tit. And you promised us some action.'

'You'll get some action when our man arrives,' replied Hobson, sensing immediately a wave of curiosity sweeping over from the back of the car. This was the first mention of a man who was due to arrive.

'What man?' asked Joe.

Hobson was reluctant to specify him by name. It seemed to provoke curious responses from people, both uniformed and civilian, but having come thus far, it seemed pointless to withhold the information from his volunteers.

'I know him as Big Al.'

The immediate reaction was five minutes of near-hysterical laughter. An enterprising television company should have recorded it. With skilful editing and multi-tracking it would have provided studio audience accompaniment for a hundred years of situation comedy pro-grammes and game shows.

By ten past seven they had calmed down sufficiently to explain the reasons for their laughter. Briefly summarized, these were that the force had suspected Big Al for months but figured he was too smart to be nicked and would probably have to be set up. There was also a minority theory that the man was honest.

Hobson made it clear that corruption was not in his plan of campaign, nor in his nature.

'Then you've no chance,' said Joe.

It was only by pulling rank that Hobson was able to persuade his volunteers to continue the surveillance, plus a promise that he would personally guarantee their overtime claim from his own pocket if necessary.

At seven-thirty the meeting in support of Jill Swinburne's election campaign was due to start. The audience still consisted of Trevor Chaplin.

'Tell you what. Start your speech and maybe the room'll fill up once you get going.'

The response was an armour-piercing glare. He shrugged his shoulders and started to make a paper aeroplane from an election leaflet.

At seven-thirty, Big Al cycled up to the door of St Matthew's church, opened it and entered. Hobson sat forward, eagerly. Joe and Ben took no notice. They were deep in a copy of *Sporting Life*.

'Three ... two ... one ... zero!' said Hobson.

'What sort of talk's that?' asked Joe, as Hobson started the car and accelerated fast towards the church.

The three policemen got out of the car, and walked with variable enthusiasm towards the huge oak doors.

'I hope you don't want it smashing open,' said Joe.

'We will open the door and walk in, quietly and sensibly,' replied Sergeant Hobson, sounding more like a first class graduate than ever. He did as promised, and was followed into the church by Joe and Ben.

Big Al was waiting for them, a smile on his face.

'Hello, lads,' he said to Joe and Ben. 'Good evening, sergeant,' he said to Hobson. He put his finger to his lips. 'Don't make a row. The vicar's in the organ loft. He's just going to have a quick toccata and fugue. He generally does that on a Friday. Did you want something?'

'Yes, please,' said Hobson, 'a look around the basement.'

'Certainly,' said Big Al, with a flourish and a slight bow. 'We keep the basement downstairs.'

He led Hobson and his volunteers down the spiral staircase, opening the door on to the treasure house that lived in the vaults.

Sergeant Hobson spied the possibility of glory, promotion and a distinction in his thesis. No man could possibly gather together such a galaxy of consumer goods without breaking the law, or at least straining it at the seams. He picked up a kettle.

'Can you explain this?'

'It's a kettle. We're looking after it for my brother. There's the receipt.'

He handed Hobson a receipt from one of several bulging files on a desk nearby. Hobson checked it. It was genuine.

'The wheelbarrow?'

'We're looking after it for my sister. There's the receipt.'

'The vacuum cleaner?'

'We're looking after it for me. There's the receipt.'

The police raid was over by seven forty-five. Every item in the basement had a receipt and a cover story. Big Al also had a letter from the vicar, giving permission for the storage of goods in the basement. Joe and Ben had terminal hysterics.

Hobson had a developing theory. If he wanted to nail Big Al, he would have to set him up.

And Big Al had the last line. As Hobson climbed into the car a voice called to him from the gathering gloom.

'You need better informants, sergeant. Your grass is a bit green.'

At seven forty-five Trevor and Jill agreed that the prospect of an audience for her meeting was receding faster than a neurotic executive's hairline.

'I'll check outside for latecomers,' said Jill, fighting back the agony of political despair.

'And if anybody turns up here, I'll keep them talking till you get back.'

Jill made her way along marbled corridors and down an elaborate staircase, scanning the stray potters and flat-earthers for the merest suggestion of a frustrated concern for the environment. Outside the building the street was deserted. Democracy had betrayed her, very likely for a documentary on Channel Four. As she turned to go into the Institute, she stared. The large poster outside, advertising the meeting, bore a supplementary sticker. On it, in large red letters, was written: CANCELLED OWING TO ILLNESS.

The plot was amazingly simple. This was the promised explosion. The major event of her election campaign had been ruined by a device of childlike simplicity.

She stormed up the stairs, along the corridor, and into Room 17A.

'I have been cancelled owing to illness!' she exclaimed.

Then she realized that Trevor was not alone. He was talking to an attractive, dark-haired girl.

'I'm sorry,' said Jill, 'do I have an audience?'

Trevor Chaplin smiled, shrugged and shuffled.

'Not exactly. This is ... er ... that is ... I'd like you to meet ... Helen of Tadcaster.'

Four

It used to be said that there were a million stories in the naked city of New York.

Just after ten past eight on an average early summer evening in the outer limits of Leeds, there might be a few hundred; on this particular evening there were at least three, two mobile and one static.

In a yellow van, Trevor Chaplin was driving Jill Swinburne home, following an abortive election meeting, and accompanied by Helen of Tadcaster, his lost love. Jill had invited her to join them for coffee and a chat. Trevor was fearful of the chat.

In a plain police car, Detective Sergeant Hobson, BA, was driving back to the police station, following an abortive raid on the parish church of St Matthew, in search of stolen property. He was accompanied by his volunteers, the recalcitrant double act Joe and Ben, who knew he had perpetrated a cock-up and would take full advantage of the moral superiority inherent in the situation.

Sitting on the steps of the parish church of St Matthew, Big Al and Little Norm were reflecting on the implications of the police raid. Norm had turned up, ready for an hour's brisk stock-taking, to see the departure of the constabulary.

'Did they find anything?'

'Don't be daft, Norm. I blinded them with science and invoices.'

'So there's no problem.'

Al adjusted the angle of his cap to shield his eyes against the setting sun, which was diving in low and hard across the gables of The Swinging Hod, a pub much favoured by artisans from the building trade, when there was such a thing in the district.

'I don't like being noticed,' said Al, 'most of all by that birdbrain Hobson. I think we should sit here for a bit and worry.'

They sat on the church steps and worried.

In the plain police car, Hobson was worried, too. The silence from Joe and Ben was dense with cynical condemnation. He decided on a pre-emptive strike.

'Let's be quite clear about this. I do not regard this evening's operation as a failure.'

'Huh?'

'In fact, I would regard the operation as a success.'

'Huh??'

'I admit, we carried out a raid on a church, looking for stolen property, and we found no stolen property. But it has enabled us to eliminate one vital element in the inquiry.'

'Huh???'

'We know now that the property in the church basement is not stolen.' As he said it, he realized he was whistling a feeble tune, offkey in a hostile darkness.

'With respect, sir,' said Joe, indicating he had no respect at all for the person addressed, 'we've told you how to nick Big Al.'

'I do not frame people!'

Joe ignored him and continued with his street-wise thesis. 'Set him up. Plant some evidence and knock him off.'

Hobson played what he assumed to be the trump card.

'And what about Superintendent Forrest?'

Joe and Ben nodded in unison.

'Obviously,' said Ben, 'you don't set people up until you've cleared it with Mr Forrest.'

Sergeant Hobson opted out of further debate on the subject of Big Al. He was a stranger in a strange land, where the natives spoke differently, lived by a different moral code and where citizens, honest or otherwise, were apparently framed on criminal charges with the authority of the station superintendent. Hitherto, he had assumed that Forrest was rough but straight. Where was the craggy Northern integrity he had read about in those 1960s novels? Was *Z Cars* pure mythology? When in Rome, was it absolutely compulsory to do as the Romans did?

Trevor made the coffee, while Jill and Helen sat in the executive through-lounge and talked about him. Jill was keen to grasp the essentials of the story so far.

'According to Trevor, you two were once engaged, and you quit because he was boring you out of your skull? Is that about right?'

'That's about right,' agreed Helen.

The two women were smiling and sparring. Helen's arrival at the meeting that never was had taken Jill by surprise. Trevor's easy familiarity with Jill and her house had taken Helen by surprise. He knew where to find coffee, milk, sugar and cups. She wondered whether he was equally familiar with the upstairs geography of the house and, for that matter, with the geography of Jill herself.

'Have you two known each other long?' she asked Jill, with a casual look that, transformed into electricity, would have provided heat, light and energy for a town the size of Swindon.

Jill explained about the breakup of her marriage two

years earlier, how Trevor had started giving her lifts to school, and how a bottle of Frascati had brought them closer together. 'A relationship developed.'

The phrase hit the room like the clanging of a bell.

'You mean . . . sex and things?' asked Helen.

'Yes. Sex and things.'

'Great.'

Helen's apparent approval of the sex and things carried all the passionate enthusiasm of a *Michelin Guide* inspector confronted with a jumbo cheeseburger and double chips.

'Also I'm very good about the house,' added Trevor, as he walked through from the kitchen with a tray loaded with coffee and biscuits.

'The two of you live together?'

This was a difficult question to answer. Some of the time they lived together and some of the time they lived separately. There was a silent and mutual understanding whereby every so often Trevor would stay at his flat for a few days, generally to listen his way through the latest batch of jazz records. Additionally, they had agreed to maintain their independent lives. People should not live together unless they were equally capable of living alone. It was a beguiling concept, which Jill had read about in *The Guardian*. Explaining it in two sentences to the male partner's ex-fiancée was a trickier proposition, and they both evaded the problem.

'More or less,' said Trevor.

'Sort of,' said Jill.

'I see,' said Helen.

They sipped coffee and nibbled Garibaldis in silence for a while, before Helen tried another question.

'It isn't easy, Jill, but I have to ask you . . . how important is Trevor to you?'

Jill felt like the contestant in a quiz show, shut in

the glass booth, knowing that a major prize hung on her ability to find the answer in ten seconds, starting from now. She observed her habit of a lifetime and told the truth.

'Half the time he drives me mad. Half the time he keeps me sane.'

'Obviously he hasn't changed.'

Trevor, weary of being discussed like a laboratory specimen exploded at the two women: 'Well, I'm very sorry, but I'm all I've got!'

'This is our business, Trevor, you just pour some more coffee,' said Helen.

He looked from one to the other, in near-terminal perplexity, then directed his words at Helen. 'When you said that ... this is our business, Trevor, you pour some more coffee ... you sounded just like *her*!' He wheeled round and glared at Jill.

'So?' said Jill.

He shrugged. 'I'll pour some more coffee.'

Big Al and Little Norm were asking difficult questions of themselves as they played darts in the public bar of The Swinging Hod.

'Who shopped us?' said Al, scoring a hundred with three darts, flung harpoon style.

'How did the police know to search the basement?' said Norm, throwing his darts with a limp-wristed elegance modelled on the style of the recent winner of a major television championship. Norm's first two darts scored eleven between them and the third hit the lamp above the board before bouncing halfway across the room, where it almost skewered the foot of an itinerant navvy and dedicated Guinness drinker who turned with an irate: 'Who done that?'

'He done that,' said Big Al, stepping up to take his throw.

The navvy realized Al was strong, tall, muscular and a master of grammar and syntax. He picked up the dart and handed it to Norm. 'This is yours, I believe, sir.'

'Ta,' said Norm.

Big Al assessed the scoreboard. 'Hundred and seven needed for game. I make that treble seventeen, single twenty and double eighteen. A neat finish combining beauty and logic in equal measure.'

He threw the darts into the treble seventeen, single twenty and double eighteen.

'Right. That's finished my game of bowls. Now let's work out who shopped us to the King of Spain.'

Al sat down in the domino corner, while Norm pulled up a stool to join him, and tried to work out what the King of Spain had to do with it.

'You're always talking about three things at once,' he moaned to Al, who ignored him.

'Who knows about the basement?'

'Er . . .' said Norm, before Al continued.

'You, me, the vicar, Mrs Swinburne and Trev Chaplin. That's who knows about the basement and none of them would shop us, therefore it must have been person or persons unknown. And nearly everything is about three things at once, including life itself, Norm.'

Little Norm shuffled the dominoes idly. 'What about sex?' he suggested.

'You look more like you fancied a game of dominoes.'

'No, what I mean is, you say life's generally about three things at once. Whereas sex, as far as I can remember, when you're having it, is about one thing at once.'

'You think that, do you, old son?'

'Yes.'

'No wonder you live in a state of permanent confusion.'

'I don't. Do I?' inquired Little Norm.

'I agree with you,' said Al. 'Let's have a game of dommies.'

As darkness falls over the suburban sections of the outer limits, curtains are closed with firmness and precision along all the avenues, closes and crescents, with the exception of Jill Swinburne's house. After the departure of her ex-husband, she decided that, like Sweden, she would have no secrets from the world. Since life in her through-lounge was generally undramatic, it was a pretty nominal gesture, and if there were the odd moment of unbridled passion, she was content for the passing stroller to observe and revel in the cheap thrill, if his or her taste lay in that direction.

Tonight there were no cheap thrills in evidence. The light from the picture window framed a domestic scene of awesome cosiness. Trevor was wedged in a corner of the settee, sleeping peacefully, while Jill sat in close and intimate conversation with Helen of Tadcaster.

It was a scene of no great consequence to the average voyeur, and yet they were watched. In a car parked across the street sat a man wearing dark glasses.

The two women had no idea they were under surveillance. Jill was absorbed in Helen's blow-by-blow account of her early life with Trevor.

'We got engaged, started saving money in a building society, bought sheets and towels. Then I decided we were boring. Both of us. So I broke off the engagement and ran away to London where the streets are paved with blokes.'

'And I bet you met one.'

Helen nodded, and Jill nodded too. They both understood the slings and arrows, the sorrow and the pity, the vales of tears implicit in the phrase: met a bloke.

Helen described hers.

'He was one of the million and a half blokes in London who tell you they work in the media. Sharp suit and forward-facing haircut. Suave as buggery.'

'Did it end in tears?'

'Yes,' said Helen, 'he cried his eyes out. I got the next train home. Came back to Mummy and Daddy.'

There was in Helen's voice a distant echo of elocution lessons, and in her clothing a hint of high-limit credit cards. Jill wondered what Daddy did that made all this possible.

'Forgive my asking, but what does Daddy do? And is he good at it?'

'He has chemists' shops.'

'Many?'

'Enough. And a few other things besides.'

Jill was reassured in her judgement. She had caught a whiff of loot and was right. She was less certain about Helen's motives where Trevor was concerned, but approached the problem in her usual way, by asking the question outright.

'And having come home to Mummy and Daddy, you thought you'd check out Trevor, to see if he was still boring?'

'I suppose so.'

They turned to look at him. He was clustered in an angle of the settee, eyes closed, limbs protruding in a variety of directions like an ill-designed compass, but relaxed and tranquil, with an apparent innocence that both women knew ran through the grain of his being. They were united by an urge to protect, but aware that the rights of protection could not be shared easily. He was just a nice man, goddammit, and such were thin on the ground.

'What a pretty picture,' said Jill.

'Bless the child,' said Helen.

'Innocent and infuriating.'

'Drives you mad.'

'Keeps you sane.'

'I'm not asleep,' said Trevor quietly, without opening his eyes.

'What you heard was all lies,' said Jill, firmly.

Trevor sat up, opened his eyes, stretched all four limbs, and was suddenly wide awake, and interrogating.

'Helen. You came looking for me. How did you find me?'

'I went to the flat and you weren't there, but on your door was a poster advertising Jill's meeting at the Institute.'

'So you went to the Institute. But the poster outside had a sticker on saying cancelled owing to illness. So why did you come in?'

Helen stared at Jill. 'Of course. You're not ill, are you?'

'No. I'm as well as can be expected in the circumstances.'

Trevor persisted. 'Answer the question, Helen. Why did you come into the meeting if the poster said the meeting was cancelled?'

'The man said you'd be there.'

'Which man?'

Neither of the women could recall such a display of incisive questioning from Trevor, or, for that matter, incisive answering. His nature and record were more in the tradition of soft answers, gentle deflections and wry ambiguity.

'You're being decisive, love,' said Jill, 'and I'm not sure we can cope with it.'

She never called him love, even at moments of abandon beneath the duvet, and in his present mood of inquiry, Trevor was keen enough to notice that too; but he was not to be diverted from the main line of investigation. 'Tell us about the man.'

Helen explained: 'When I arrived at the Institute there

was a man putting a sticker on top of the poster. The sticker said cancelled owing to illness. I said what a shame, there was somebody I wanted to see at the meeting. The man asked who it was. I told him. The man said go in and check, because you'd probably be there.'

'What did this man look like?'

'Ordinary. He had a dog with him.'

'A bloke with a dog?'

'Yes. That's why I said it.'

'Jason!' cried Trevor and Jill in unison.

The man in the dark glasses abandoned his surveillance around midnight. By then, Jill's house was in total darkness.

Helen had insisted it was time she made her way to Tadcaster. Trevor insisted on giving her a lift. Helen insisted she would take a taxi. Trevor insisted that it was no bother. Jill insisted she should stay the night. Helen stayed the night, in the spare room. None of this was overheard by the man in dark glasses, but it was almost certainly irrelevant to his purpose.

It was by no means irrelevant to Trevor Chaplin, Jill Swinburne and Helen of Tadcaster. They all three realized they were locked in a triangle, the most sinister geometric device in the history of emotion. Though they claimed at breakfast the next day to have slept soundly, it was not true.

Trevor Chaplin lay awake, eyes closed, under the duvet, thinking: I am apparently fancied by two women. Is this a record? Yes.

Alongside him, Jill Swinburne lay awake thinking: he drives me mad and he keeps me sane. How do I resolve this apparent contradiction? With difficulty.

In the spare room, Helen of Tadcaster lay awake, eyes open, staring at the unfamiliar shapes of window, walls and ceiling, thinking: Trevor is living with a woman. Is this not amazing and unpredictable? You bet it is.

Had she been totally honest, Helen might have admitted that she also listened for significant noises from the adjoining bedroom. She heard naught but the silence of chastity. In a way it was an alarming sound, because it indicated to her that Jill and Trevor had no need to prove anything.

Breakfast was unusual. Jill prepared bacon and fried bread for Trevor, instead of the usual compulsory muesli. There were two sorts of marmalade, accompanied by a deal of self-conscious banter. Helen insisted on making the coffee and the toast. Trevor did nothing except sit at the table and wallow in service.

When they were all seated, Helen laughed and said: 'It's like *Jules et Jim*.'

'It's like what?' asked Trevor.

Trevor's favourite French film was an American film called *Paris Blues* because it had a music score by Duke Ellington.

Jill explained: '*Jules et Jim* ... a film by François Truffaut ... it's about a *ménage à trois*.'

'What did Horace say, Winnie?' asked Trevor of nobody in particular. There was a race to reply, which Jill won by a short head.

'*Ménage à trois* ... three people living together ... two fellows called Jules et Jim ...'

'And a girl called Catherine,' added Helen.

Trevor bit into his toast and summarized the plot: 'Did she like two different sorts of marmalade?'

'You've got no soul!' said Jill.

'Where I was born we were too poor to have souls. Some of the Catholic kids had them but ...'

'And you're prejudiced!' said Helen.

'No, I'm not, I'm just ignorant, And I'll tell you this for nothing, Helen, you do sound like her at times.'

He grinned from one to the other. He could not imagine a *ménage à trois* as a permanent element in his life, but as a temporary arrangement he found it exhilarating.

After breakfast, Helen telephoned Daddy, or somebody who worked for Daddy, and within minutes a small Mercedes arrived to take her home to Tadcaster. Jill and Trevor waved her out of sight, then climbed into the van and headed South, towards secondary education. As usual, Jill took him by surprise.

'I really like Helen.'

Trevor had assumed that since the two women were, in his simple-minded analysis, competing for his mind and body in either order, friendliness and warmth between them were unlikely prospects. Not so, apparently. He decided to play for time.

'Good. She always knew a lot about French films.'

'I enjoyed talking to her. I think she'll make a really good friend.'

'Is that why you asked her to stay the night?'

'No.'

The negative was firm and precise, like a vintage Rod Laver backhand.

'Oh.'

'I asked her to stay the night because the alternative was for you to give her a lift to Tadcaster. That was not a good idea.'

He realized the conversation was drifting into those areas of emotion, sensitivity, feelings, motivations and relationship-related topics where he invariably floundered like a beached whale. It was not his natural habitat, but somehow it tempted him. Keeping off the grass was safe but dull. He took a careful step on to the verge.

'Why was it not a good idea for me to take Helen home?'

'Because she's extremely vulnerable at the moment.'

He shrugged. 'I'm vulnerable all the time.'

'Yes. That was the other reason.'

Trevor Chaplin guessed he was no longer at the apex of the triangle. He had a very shrewd idea who was. It was odd, because Jill always claimed that power corrupted, yet she was pretty adept at wielding it. He considered another shrug, then decided not to bother.

When Hobson arrived at the police station he noticed that the plastic name-plate on his office door reading: DET. SGT. HOBSON had been embellished with the letters BA in a thick, blue, felt-tipped scrawl. His immediate prime suspects were Joe and Ben. The writing had their childish simplicity, and between them he calculated they could just about cope with the spelling.

He did not bother looking for them. Their professional zeal stopped well short of a nine o'clock arrival. He was aware that the assembled ranks in the general office were watching for his reactions and he was determined to offer them nothing. He went into his room and closed the door on the sudden explosion of coarse, unfeeling laughter.

It was a typical, lonely start to Hobson's day. A solitary idealist floating in a dead sea of scepticism and corruption, he nonetheless relished his alienation.

To steal a phrase from their limited vocabulary: he would show the bastards. But first, he knew, as night follows day and ebb follows flow, his arrival would be followed by the ringing of the telephone.

The telephone rang. He picked up the receiver.

'Hobson.'

'Forrest.'

'Coming, sir.'

Superintendent Forrest was concerned about the abortive raid on the parish church of St Matthew, concerned to the point of hysteria.

'It's a monumental disaster. A cock-up of staggering magnitude.'

'I would freely admit an error of judgement, sir.'

'You don't have to admit anything, Hobson, I am telling you.'

'Though I would also claim that the fault was in the timing. The operation, on reflection, was ill-timed.'

Forrest grabbed the phrase eagerly, seeing new possibilities of verbal abuse.

'Ill-timed? Explain that, Hobson!'

'Ill-timed in the sense that the property we found was not, in point of fact, stolen property. Were we to raid the basement at the right moment, I am sure we might well find property that is, in point of fact, stolen.'

'Good God, son, you could raid all sorts of places on that basis. The Lord Mayor's parlour. Your neighbourhood convent. The Oxfam shop. Kick the place to pieces and then say sorry, everybody, we didn't find any knocked-off gear, because the raid was ill-timed. Oh dear, oh lor' ...'

Forrest poured himself a drink from the coffee pot, added ice and soda, took a deep breath, then launched into another monologue, this time with a disarmingly gentle tone.

'Look, son, you think I've got it in for you because you're a graduate copper. You think it's arse-about-face snobbery because you've got first class honours and I've got a Liverpool accent.'

For a a moment, Hobson felt a rush of compassion for his commanding officer. He was confessing to deep and complex feelings and the younger man responded accordingly.

'No, sir, I don't think that, truly I don't.'

'Good lad!' roared Forrest. 'Because it isn't that, it's purely personal! I just don't like you! And you're useless at the job! Resentment about your education and upbringing has nothing to do with it. Understood?'

'I understand, sir.'

'Right. Sling your hook.'

Hobson began to sling his hook, but when he was half-way to the door, Forrest called him back.

'Hang on a minute, wonder boy. There is something else you omitted to tell me. You omitted to tell me as it was Big Al you were trying to nick.'

'Ah ...'

'There is only one way to nick Big Al. It is a well known scientific fact.'

Hobson tried a new approach: playing to what he assumed to be the gallery.

'Plant some evidence and fit him up?' he suggested, with a careful combination of brightness and a sardonically raised left eyebrow. Forrest stared at him, face revealing tabloid-style shock and horror, as if he had personally discovered the vicar and the cub mistress in their secret love-nest.

'Hobson, I am astonished to hear such a suggestion fall from your lips. We never plant evidence and we never fit people up.'

'No, sir. Sorry, sir. A flippant jest, sir.'

'Except in one very precise situation that does not at this moment arise.'

'When might that be, sir?' asked Hobson, with an eager-to-learn tilt of the head.

'We set people up when I order it to be done. In Big Al's case I am giving no such orders. There is such a thing as integrity, Hobson, even in this age of rock and roll.'

'I find that very reassuring, sir,' said Hobson.

'Well you would, being, as you are, round the bend. That's all. I may decide to shout at you again later.'

Hobson returned to his room. While he reorganized the

index system of his PhD research files, he brooded on the moral complexities of the police force around him. Joe and Ben had recommended setting up Big Al as a normal prerequisite of an early arrest. Superintendent Forrest appeared to endorse this principle. But was he joking? Were Joe and Ben teasing him? He found it impossible to penetrate the Northern approach to humour. These people with their flat vowels and arbitrary consonants found amusement in the strangest subjects: death, destruction, illness, social deprivation, emotional despair and the warping of truth. They were only serious about matters of startling triviality: dog food, motor car maintenance, bookmakers' odds and the Yorkshire cricket club committee.

Hobson could not contemplate joining them. Therefore he would have to beat them. But how and where to start? He smiled a crooked smile, aiming at a lean and hungry look. Sergeant Hobson, BA, was an ambitious man and maybe he should have his sights on the biggest bastard available. He loaded a new, blank tape into his recorder.

It was lunch as usual in the canteen at San Quentin High. Trevor's potatoes were cold, Jill's lettuce was warm and Mr Carter was grumbling.

'I asked for our regular corner table, between the orchestra and the potted palms, and here we are, marooned in a sea of gravy once more.'

Trevor and Jill ignored him, also as usual. He decided on a more direct approach.

'How was your meeting last night, Mrs Swinburne?'

'Non-existent. Nobody turned up.'

At that moment a large boy marched into the dining hall and across to their table. Bradley was an amiable youth of very little brain but immense goodwill. The professional judgement of the staff was that he might scrape an O-level in shoelace-tying if he was allowed to use a crib, and thereafter he should write to the Dean of York Minster, applying for a job as a buttress.

He stood behind Trevor, silently indicating that he had information to convey.

'You're being loomed over,' said Jill.

'What do you want, son?' asked Trevor.

Bradley concentrated hard. People usually gave him notes. Verbal messages he found more arduous. 'Sir. My brother wants to see you. Sir. In the woodwork room. Sir. Now, please. Sir.'

'Well done, Bradley!' said Mr Carter. It was the longest continuous speech he had ever heard from the boy.

Trevor was equally impressed, but puzzled by one aspect of the message. 'Didn't realize you had a brother,' he said.

'No, sir. I haven't. Only sisters. Loads of sisters.'

Trevor stood up. 'In that case, I'd better not keep your brother waiting.'

Bradley ambled after Trevor in the general direction of the woodwork room, then remembered that he had completed his mission and could proceed with his everyday life. Through the window of the dining hall, he spotted a playground soccer match in ferocious progress: nineteen-a-side and very little evidence of a ball. While Bradley concentrated on working out a route to take him from canteen to football pitch, Mr Carter was trying to clarify the logic of the conversation he had witnessed.

'Do I understand it that Mr Chaplin has gone to speak to the brother of a boy who does not have a brother?'

'Yes,' said Jill, 'it's obvious enough to me.'

'Forgive my simple mind, Mrs Swinburne, but when Mr Chaplin walks into the woodwork room, who is likely to be there?'

'Big Al.'

'As you say, it is obvious.'

It was obvious to Trevor, too, and he discovered Al taking a keen interest in the stockpile of table lamps, book-ends and tea pot stands that marked out the boundaries of the Chaplin career.

For once Al was silent. He carried on with his inspection, then turned to look at Trevor. He regarded him. He contemplated him. He reflected upon him. Then he spoke.

'No, I don't think so.'

'Pardon?'

'There's no way you could be a police informer. I apologize for even thinking about it, Trev.'

'No need to apologize. I've no idea what you're talking about.'

Al outlined the reason for his visit. He explained about the police raid, and how only five people knew about the basement. He had worked his way down the list: himself, Little Norm, the vicar, Mrs Swinburne and Trev. It was logical that one of the five must have tipped off Sergeant Hobson. But it was equally logical that none of the five would have tipped off the police because all five were truthful, honest, of good report and what's more Al looked upon all of them as brothers, with the exception of Mrs Swinburne, whom he regarded as a sister.

'You see, Trev, there's nothing bent about that stuff in the warehouse. But I don't like people *knowing* about it. It's the intrusion on our privacy that gets up our nose.'

'Difficult, because I haven't a clue what a police informer looks like,' said Trevor.

'Nor me.'

'Yes I do!' Trevor's eyes sparkled. 'I think our police informer looks like a man with a dog!'

'A man with a dog?'

'I know the man and I know the dog.'

'Do you know his name?' asked Big Al.

'Jason.'

'And what's the feller called?'

Sergeant Hobson, having satisfied himself that Superintendent Forrest was likely to be pursuing urgent inquiries on the golf course all afternoon, was in his office, sharing insight with his tape recorder.

'I cannot believe that a basement warehouse in a parish church, crammed to the rafters . . .' He stopped the tape, rewound it and started again: 'I cannot believe that a church basement, crammed to its brick, barrel-vaulted ceiling with consumer goods, is not a sign of criminal activity. Its very abnormality must inevitably signal a breach of the law, whether criminal, moral or civil, and perhaps all three.'

He stopped the tape. Like Trevor in the woodwork room, he spotted a revelation on the road ahead. It might not be the main road to Damascus, but it was a highly promising side street.

Twenty minutes later, Sergeant Hobson stepped briskly and optimistically through the stately portals of the town hall. It took him another twenty minutes to attract anybody's attention at the Inquiry counter, twenty-five minutes to find the room he was directed to, but only five minutes to discover the information he was seeking.

He emerged from the town hall smiling.

One of the repeating patterns of life with Jill Swinburne took place each day at home, immediately on their return from school. Trevor would make a pot of China tea, which he loathed, pending their evening meal at seven, while Jill would make many telephone calls. Trevor ignored these because he could hear only half of the conversation and the subjects were in the general area of resolutions and agendas, which he found fascinating, but not very.

He was pouring the tea as Jill hung up the receiver and called across to him: 'We're being taken out to dinner tonight.'

'Who by?'

'Your ex-girlfriend. Helen. We're going to one of Daddy's restaurants.'

'Thought he had chemists' shops.'

'She's picking us up in one of Daddy's cars at seven.'

'Great. But I'm not coming.'

Jill was not pleased to learn that Trevor had a prior engagement, especially when he revealed that his matter of high priority was a trip with Big Al to do some heavy lifting. His refusal to give any further details did not help the case. Nor was Helen thrilled beyond measure when she arrived in a medium-sized Mercedes with power-assisted door handles and push-button buttons, when she saw Trevor dressed in his standard heavy-lifting uniform of Sunderland football club tee-shirt and jeans.

'Trevor! You can't come out with us looking like that!'

'Not coming,' said Trevor. 'Sorry. I'm helping a mate cleanse the world of all evil. Heyup, is that the time?'

As Trevor crossed to the door, he handed an after-thought to Helen, who was still gazing at him, stunned by his cavalier rejection of a free meal.

'I didn't know your father had restaurants.'

'I keep telling you, Trevor, things change. He was taken rich.'

'But he's still got chemists' shops?'

'He's got the chemists' shops, and a few other bits of things. Bits of supermarkets. Bits of hotels. Bits of York-shire.'

Jill was putting her coat on, and paused with left arm in mid-sleeve: 'Bits of Yorkshire?'

'Farms,' explained Helen, smiling. There was no compelling reason to frown when Daddy owned bits of Yorkshire.

The three of them walked down the path together. Trevor climbed into the van and headed in the direction of Big Al's. The medium-sized Mercedes set off towards a pretty town on a river, twenty miles distant, on the edge of the celebrated Yorkshire Dales. Jill sat in awe of the dashboard and suggested the agenda for the evening.

'That settles it. We'll have to talk about Trevor behind his back.'

'Always the best way.'

Jill pressed a button, tentatively, in search of Radio 4, and the roof slid open.

In many and various quarters of the outer limits, people were dressed up for the evening, whether for work or play or, in Harry's case, dog-walking. He usually wore the same raincoat and cap, but always cleaned his shoes prior to the evening walk. This was to remove the detritus of the afternoon walk.

Most evenings, Harry and Jason trod the bounds of the Alderman Wotsisname Memorial Playing Fields. There was fresh air to be found here, the spring of the turf beneath the feet, and a sprinkling of dog-walkers who, if they were not on their guard, might be drawn into conversation on Harry's favourite topic: what a lousy day today was compared with yesterday but not to worry, tomorrow would be even worse.

Harry scanned the playing fields in search of conversational quarry. There was not a dog-walker to be seen, not even a stray unaccompanied terrier or whippet. What he saw surprised but did not alarm him. Two football pitches away was a little yellow van. At first Harry assumed it was some kind of mirage or optical illusion. His inadequate eyesight had served the purpose of keeping him out of the army in 1941, and forty-odd years spent in concentrated study of football pools and racing pages had not improved it.

But even Harry could tell when a yellow van started its engine and accelerated across football pitches in his direction. He was bound to assume that he and the van were in some way connected. He was not worried. He did not consider flight. There was nowhere to run, and fleetness of foot was never one of his assets.

He stood quite still, mildly quizzical, as the van drew up beside him. He did not even protest when Big Al and Trevor Chaplin emerged from the van, grabbed him by an arm apiece, and bundled him into it. He protested, carefully, when Little Norm took Jason's lead and, inevitably, Jason too, from him.

'What you doing?'

'Shut it,' said Little Norm, slamming the back doors of the van in Harry's face. Trevor and Al climbed into the front seats.

'Cuba?' said Trevor.

'Tolpuddle Street.'

'Am I being kidnapped?' asked Harry.

'That's right,' said Al.

'Good. I like to know what's going on.'

Little Norm watched as the van drove quickly away across the football pitches before zooming left behind the blackened shell of the burnt-out cricket pavilion. Then he turned to Jason, who sat at the end of his lead, one ear cocked, tail wagging warily.

'Come on, boy,' said Norm, 'me and you are going to take a walk.'

*

Sergeant Hobson was already noted by his colleagues as a snappy dresser. They hated him for it; the silver-grey suits, the cut-throat creases, the white shirts that dazzled on a sunny day, the impeccably knotted ties which were either tasteful or old school, and sometimes both. In their view, plain-clothes men should wear plain clothes. If they insisted on dressing like advertising executives or television interviewers, how could the public tell they were detectives?

Even so, Hobson had smartened himself up a notch or two this summer evening, not because he was eating at a fancy restaurant in a pretty riverside town, and not because he was taking his dog for a walk. Sergeant Hobson was going to church.

He was paying a marginally off-duty visit to the parish of St Matthew. He was uncertain whether the call was official or unofficial, because he had taken the collective hints from Ben, Joe and Superintendent Forrest that the best-laid schemes of any ace detective in this area were those where the investigating officer kept every last detail tightly locked inside his skull. Henceforth, Hobson was walking alone, accepting the truth that on the whole nobody was very keen to walk with him.

He pushed open the door of the church. As arranged earlier with a discreet telephone call, the Reverend Booth was waiting for him, by the font.

The clergyman was in his early thirties and resigned to being described as a trendy vicar. His experiences while marching, demonstrating, picketing and defending civil liberties had left his Christian principles intact, but he was disinclined to turn the other cheek where policemen were concerned. He usually covered his head and went limp, and saved the other cheek for a future occasion.

However, one sight of Sergeant Hobson reassured him that the cheek might be safely revealed.

'Reverend Booth? Detective Sergeant Hobson.'

A handshake, firm but not intimidating, as might precede a charity cricket match between actors and jockeys. Hobson looked up and away, eyes sparkling with curiosity.

'What marvellous stained glass!'

Booth smiled and was comforted; they always said nice things about the stained glass, even though a third of the panes were broken and the Victorians who had made it had wilfully misinterpreted the gospels to portray the ruling classes in a celestial light.

'Yes, we're quite proud of it.'

'But I didn't come here to discuss stained glass.'

'I expect you came to discuss the basement,' said Booth, who had written to the chief constable that morning, complaining about the raid.

'Yes,' said Hobson. He hesitated, feeling curiously small and irrelevant in the cold vastness of this huge church that had clearly outlived its usefulness. 'Mind if I sit down?'

'Take a pew,' said Booth.

They sat down at the back of the orchestra stalls.

'A simple and direct question, minister. Do you trust Big Al?'

'In my trade, I have to trust everybody. It's in the book.'

'Alas,' said Hobson, 'I have to work with a different book.'

Booth outlined his gospel on the matter of Big Al. The man was doing useful work for the community, and operating strictly within the law. The police raid had proved it to be so.

'I realize it is your professional responsibility to be suspicious, Sergeant Hobson, but I am quite satisfied that storing goods in the church basement breaks no law, whether criminal, civil or moral.'

'Have you checked the town planning regulations?'

asked Hobson, with a smile of English gentlemanly triumph.

'Oh God!' said the vicar. He knew when he was beaten.

The outer limits are a monument to the Industrial Revolution, but drive twenty miles to the West and there is a pretty town spanning the banks of a gently flowing river. At weekends the streets are packed with merry artisans and their families, with the recently redundant using up their severance payment, with American tourists en route for James Herriott's autograph. Such people need food and drink, and the entrepreneurial spirit that in the nineteenth century built the mill chimneys today buys up the prime sites, transforming the old stone buildings into bistro, pizzaria and chop suey wine bar.

Of that ilk was the Taverna Pigalle, part-owned by Helen of Tadcaster's Daddy. He had chosen the name himself, arguing that it would appeal to lovers of both French and Italian food, plus macho Northern males who, misreading the word Taverna, would grasp the essential fact that here was a place they could get pissed, albeit at a price.

Helen and Jill sat at a table overlooking the river, picking their way through the complexities of the menu, printed in simulated handwriting on large sheets of glossy card. They had been discussing the challenge for twenty minutes, and were still choosing their starters.

'Don't forget,' said Helen, 'Daddy's paying.'

'That makes it easier to decide. Let's have a bottle of champagne for starters.'

They ordered a bottle of champagne and from there on the decisions became much easier.

There was no champagne for Harry, huddled on an upturned beer crate in Al's shed, flanked by the big man and Trevor Chaplin. The reason for the kidnapping was filtering through to him, though separation from Jason was a greater anxiety.

Al leaned closer to him, almost nose-to-nose, and Harry forgot his dog completely.

'Now listen, sunbeam. The reason you're here is dead simple. We want to know three things. Who told the police we were storing things in the basement of the church? Who sabotaged Mrs Swinburne's election meeting? Who smashed up my greenhouse?'

Harry remembered a phrase from a documentary he had seen, once upon a time, about the McCarthy hearings in the USA. 'I have nothing to say on account of I don't want to incriminate myself.'

'You'll regret your silence,' said Big Al. He straightened up to almost his full height. It was virtually impossible for him to stand up totally straight because of the assortment of watering cans, buckets and tools slung from the low roof of the shed. Al winked at Trevor, who had no idea what the wink signified. He soon found out.

'The way this operation works,' explained Al, 'is like this. I'm the gentle persuader. My friend here is the hard man. He's a Geordie and you know what bastards they can be.' Al wandered across to the door. 'I'll go outside for ten minutes, while he does the necessary.'

Al opened the door and left the shed. Harry turned fearfully to Trevor, obviously wondering what constituted the necessary, where the prising out of information was concerned. Trevor was wondering the same thing.

'Right. Three questions,' said Trevor, playing for time.

'He said that.'

'I know he said that!' barked Trevor, hoping that raising his voice might act as an intimidating element.

There was an uneasy silence. Harry was silent because

he clearly expected the grievous bodily harm that Al had warned him about. Trevor was silent because inflicting even trivial bodily harm was not in his nature, and therefore he had never bothered learning how to do it.

He followed the logic of his own dilemma while crossing to the window, trying to look as if he was pondering a choice between thumbscrews and boiling oil. Then Harry, embarrassed by the silence, came to the rescue.

'I hope Jason's all right,' he said.

'Oh yes, he's in good hands,' replied Trevor, suddenly inspired. He smiled, trying to make it look fairly evil and nasty, and moved towards Harry. 'That's just it. Jason is with Little Norm, who hates dogs. He had a paper round when he was a lad, and had a lot of nasty experiences with alsatians and labradors.'

Harry protested Jason's innocence: 'Jason isn't a labrador or an alsatian. Jason isn't anything. Jason wouldn't hurt a fly.'

'But that's the way it goes, mister. It's the innocent who suffer.'

Trevor was rather pleased with that's the way it goes. He remembered a film in which a New York cop used the phrase. He also saw that Harry's everyday demeanour of tremulous defiance was crumbling. The man had given up on the world years ago, but the final crumb of love was saved for his dog. Trevor had found the answer.

'Little Norm will take it in easy stages. Every half-hour. On the hour and on the half-hour.' He checked his watch. 'I make it quarter past.'

'What'll he do to Jason?'

Trevor shrugged. It came easily. 'He'll think of something. He's had all those years since the paper round to think of something. He broods a lot, Little Norm.'

Big Al was not wasting time. He was banking a row of

potatoes when the door of the shed opened and Trevor called to him.

'He's decided to talk.'

Al stuck his fork in the ground, marking the place that he was up to, and walked across to the shed, keen to hear Harry's confession.

Little Norm, contrary to the legend invented that evening by Trevor Chaplin, quite liked dogs and had never been a paper lad. After the kidnapping of Harry, he and Jason sat on a bench overlooking the bleak acres of the Alderman Wotsisname Memorial Playing Fields, waiting for the time to pass. Norm had hoped there might be a football match but the fields remained deserted. Not even a solitary jogger or stray flasher showed up to ease the shared tedium of prisoner and captor.

Norm contemplated a walk around the playing field but he had arranged to wait by the bench for the van's return. Then he remembered. Earlier that evening, during the briefing, Al had given him an old tennis ball.

'Use that to keep the dog happy,' he had said.

Norm fished in his pocket and produced the tennis ball. It was very old and bald, and would not have been allowed past the gates at Wimbledon, but Jason was clearly free of the sin of pride. He sat up, ears pert, tail wagging.

'Fetch, Jason, fetch!' said Norm, hurling the ball as far as he could and letting go of the lead. Jason hurtled off in the direction of the tennis ball, only to ignore it completely and keep on running in the direction of Bradford. That was the last Norm saw of him.

While Jason was galloping towards Bradford, his master was making his true confession in Big Al's shed.

'Yes. I told the police about the stuff in the church basement.'

'Why?' said Al.

'I thought I might make a few bob as a supergrass. It's a way of winning back self-respect, if you make a few bob. When I was a lad there was lots of trades.'

Trevor yawned. Harry was already ankle-deep in Northern nostalgia and it might go on for days.

'Oh yes, lots of trades. There was coopers and wheelwrights and carpenters and pattern-makers and weavers and stonemasons and –'

'What were you?' said Al.

'Bookie's runner. But what with betting shops and microchips there's no call for the old trades any more. Craftsmanship's all dead and buried.'

Big Al, a redundant craftsman himself, softened towards the man, though he naturally placed the building trade above bookie's runner in the scheme of things, with police informer at the bottom of Division Four.

'Just answer our three questions,' said Al, gently.

'And it'll be better for Jason,' added Trevor, concerned that his hard man image might be tarnished by his silence and periodic yawns.

'Jason?' asked Al, who was not aware of the methods Trevor had used.

'Questions?' asked Harry, who had forgotten the questions on his journey into the happy land of cobble-stoned yesteryear.

'Who shopped us to the police? Who sabotaged Mrs Swinburne's election meeting? Who smashed up my greenhouse?'

Harry remembered the questions immediately.

'I told you the first. I went to the police. And yes, I stuck a bit of paper on the poster for the meeting, saying Mrs Swinburne was taken ill. But I didn't do the greenhouse. I like greenhouses. I remember when these hills was a mass of greenhouses and cucumber frames from top to bottom.'

Al and Trevor, in their discussions earlier, had agreed that their man was almost certainly responsible for informing the police and spoiling the election meeting. They had also agreed that greenhouse-smashing was probably beyond him, both morally and technically. The sixty-four thousand dollar question remained. Who was giving the orders to Harry? A tedious philosopher of the streets he might be, but a freelance vandal and anarchist he was not.

'Who gives you the orders?' said Big Al.

'Bloke in the betting shop. Don't know his name.'

'Who gives him his orders?'

'Bloke on the phone. Don't know his name neither.'

'Do you know anybody's name?'

'No.'

Having ordered champagne for starters, Helen and Jill stayed loyal through main course and dessert. By the time the coffee arrived, they were in a mood for giggly reflections on the nature of love, starting with a toast.

'Absent friend.'

'Absent friend.'

They drank to Trevor, then Helen suggested another good cause.

'True love.'

'True love,' responded Jill.

They laughed. The glasses were empty. The bottle was empty too. A waiter appeared, as from a concealed trap-door, bearing a new bottle in a fresh bucket of ice. Jill smiled at the new bottle: 'Hello, good evening and welcome.'

The waiter topped up their glasses, then disappeared

down the trapdoor. The muzak seemed to be playing two tunes at once: 'Viva España' and 'I Did It My Way'.

'Daddy!' said Jill, suddenly.

'Where?'

'No, not here. I mean if he's paying for all this, we should drink a toast to your Daddy. I've never met him but I think he's truly wonderful.'

They touched glasses.

'Daddy!'

'Daddy!'

In the shed, Harry was improvising on a theme of men with no names.

'All I know is there's people that don't like what you're doing,' he said to Al.

'We're providing a valuable community service. We've re-invented the Co-op movement. Ask the vicar.'

'These people, they like people to buy things from proper shops. They like people to vote for people in proper parties like Conservative and Labour and TCP. They like people to be normal. They don't like cranks. That's why they smash up greenhouses and election meetings.'

Harry sat back to take a breather and almost slid off his beer crate, but Trevor steadied him with an outstretched arm. He transformed the Samaritan-like gesture into an apparent threat by briefly grasping the lapel of Harry's coat.

'We still want the name of one of these people. Don't forget. Jason!'

Trevor let go of Harry, in case he was hurting him.

'All right, I'll give you a name. I heard the bloke in the betting shop one day when he was on the phone and he said something like, "That's all right, Mr McAllister."'

'McAllister?' said Al. 'What is he, this McAllister?'

134

'Some sort of business man. Think he's got chemists' shops, something like that.'

'Hellfire!' said Trevor. Big Al turned to him.

'Do you know this McAllister?'

'Yes. He's Helen's Daddy.'

Like good, responsible, middle-class drunks, Helen and Jill took a taxi home from the Taverna Pigalle. One of Daddy's friends would collect the Mercedes the following day.

In the back of the cab, they reflected, cheerfully and woozily, on the topic they had avoided all evening.

'What about Trevor?'

'What about Trevor?'

They sat in silence, watching the dark valley slide by, and wondering: what about Trevor?

'Should we be making decisions?' asked Helen.

'Why not?' said Jill. 'It's only men who can't make decisions.'

At the time it seemed a good idea to Jill, though she was under the influence of a gargantuan free meal, extensive champagne, instant waiters, plastic carnations and piped muzak of all nations. She felt altogether grand and reckless, hearing fiercely independent voices from the annals of time: a clarion call that somehow merged Sylvia Pankhurst, Emma Goldman, Frieda Lawrence, Isadora Duncan, Jane Fonda and all points Left.

She opened her handbag and brought out a small coin of the realm. 'Heads or tails?' she asked Helen.

Helen stared, hesitated, then smiled: 'Heads.'

Jill tossed the coin, caught it, and revealed the face of their decision.

In unison the two women said: 'Hard luck.'

*

Harry was allowed to leave the shed. He was a little reluctant to go.

'I've got a question for you two.'

'We ask the questions around here,' said Trevor.

'No, listen,' said Harry, 'I've given you valuable information about Mr McAllister. How much are you going to pay me?'

'Pay you?' said Al.

'I'm thinking of becoming a double-agent.'

In unison the two investigators said: 'Shut the door as you go out.'

Harry shut the door as he went out. From the gathering gloom that shrouded the pigeon crees and gooseberry bushes of the Tolpuddle Street allotments there was a cheerful yelp. Jason galloped towards his master at maximum canine velocity. It was the happiest reunion since Lassie came home.

Five

Trevor had never seen Jill crying. It was a strange and unexpected experience. They were middle-range tears, the crying that confesses: I have drunk too much and, as a result, have been exceedingly silly. The explanation, when it arrived, took Trevor by surprise.

'I lost you.'

'Lost me? Where did you leave me? Have you looked in your other handbag?'

His flippant attitude mopped up the tears in a trice.

'We drank too much champagne, we talked about you, we tossed a coin for you, and Helen won.'

Trevor, who was eager to tell of his adventures with Big Al, of their kidnapping of Harry, the uncovering of the plot, and the emergence of Helen's father as the neighbourhood godfather, was nevertheless startled by the news.

'What did you call?' he asked.

'Heads.'

'Not a bad call, as a rule. Gives you a fifty-fifty chance.'

'But don't you realize? I have been competing. For a man!'

Trevor put a gently consoling hand on her shoulder. 'I'll make you a nice cup of tea, and we'll talk about it.'

Over tea, and a stray muffin that he had found in the kitchen, and which he ate toasted, with plum jam, he questioned Jill a little further about the implications of calling heads.

'Does this mean Helen will be beating down the door of my flat at this minute, demanding her pound of flesh?'

'No. I think she'll ring you tomorrow.'

'Next question. Do you, Jill Swinburne, want me, Trevor Chaplin, from this day forward, to have and to hold, and all that stuff?'

'Not necessarily. Now and again's quite nice.'

'All right. Try this. Do you want Helen to have me, on that basis? From this day forward etcetera?'

'Like Hell I do!'

Trevor smiled. While it was flattering to have two women draw straws over him, body and soul, Jill had brought an emotional tang to his life, only equalled by the agony of an unrequited love affair with Veronica Milburn when he was in Standard Two of his primary school in Sunderland. He expressed his passion by tying her pigtails to the chair-back. Jill had brought him richer and sweeter experiences, and in the race for his affections, Helen of Tadcaster no longer came under starter's orders.

He did not confess to any of these feelings, despite Jill's patient training. Apart from his natural inhibitions, he had a native Geordie's respect for an honestly-struck bet. If Helen had won him, then she was entitled to make some sort of gesture towards claiming the trophy; but he was not looking forward to it.

Mr Carter, a sensitive man despite what people said about him, noticed their silence in the canteen next day.

'There is a tension in the atmosphere,' he announced to Jill, Trevor and everybody within a radius of twenty yards.

'No comment,' said Jill.

'Mr Chaplin?'

'No comment,' said Trevor.

They had agreed over breakfast that Trevor should pick up his toothbrush after school and move back to his flat, until Helen made some sort of move in the direction of the major prize. They had also agreed that their public stance should be: no comment.

'In that case,' said Mr Carter, 'let me ask you this. Why is that man staring at you?'

He gestured towards the window that looked out on to the playground, which was the usual mêlée of football, rugby league, freestyle wrestling, adolescent yearning and embryonic protection rackets. Silhouetted against the window was the familiar shape of Big Al. He jerked his head briefly, somehow indicating the complete text of his message which was: I would like an immediate discussion with Trevor in the playground.

Trevor stood up.

'Excuse me. Big Al wants to see me.'

As he wandered across to the door, Mr Carter turned to Jill. 'Big Al?'

'They call him that because he's big.'

'Really.'

'And he's got a brother called Little Norm.'

Mr Carter had, by now, mastered the game.

'And I expect they call him that because he's little.'

'Yes,' said Jill, 'except he's not really Al's brother.'

Trevor and the big man circled the edge of the playground in an anti-clockwise direction, while Al outlined his problem.

'The town planners have moved in like a wolf on the fold. If we don't shift all that gear out of the church by the weekend, we're pencilled in for deportation and loss of privileges. Or a small fine.' Al, as ever, was very relaxed about the situation. He meandered through it like a philosophy don taking a stroll among his favourite concepts. 'Look at it logically, Trev. I've got a quantity of lawnmowers, refrigerators, gas cookers and similar items, and nowhere to put them. Therefore I require several hundred cubic feet of storage space, plus somebody I can trust. So I say to myself – who can I trust more than anybody in the whole world?'

They walked on in silence while Trevor considered Al's question.

'Don't know. Who?'

'You, Trev.'

'Me? But I haven't got a church basement.'

'You've got a school. You could get most of the stuff in your woodwork room.'

Trevor looked at Al, then at the undoubted cubic vastness of San Quentin High, then again at Al.

'It isn't my school.'

'It's a state school. Therefore it belongs to the people. We are the people. *Quod erat demonstrandum.*'

The lurch into Latin bothered Trevor, because he didn't know what it meant. He made a mental note to ask Jill later.

'Well, Trev?'

'It's a non-starter. It wouldn't bother me, but you'd have to clear it with the headmaster and he's a wimp. He'd want a chit from the town hall and that could take years.'

Al nodded, accepting the town hall logic.

'See what you mean. We'd never do it officially by the weekend. And do it unofficially, somebody might notice, is that what you're saying?'

'Honestly, Al, if a dozen lawnmowers suddenly appear in the woodwork room, somebody is bound to notice.'

'So it'll have to be Plan B.'

Trevor should have realized that Al's Plan B was not as innocent as it sounded.

'Plan B?'

'Share the stuff around among friends. My place, Little Norm's, Janey's, the vicarage, your flat . . .'

'Pardon?'

'Lend us your door key. I'll get a duplicate made.'

Trevor was handing his key to Big Al when the two of them almost collided with Mr Wheeler. The headmaster was circling the playground in a clockwise direction, like a German commandant keeping an eye on his stalag.

'Forgive me asking,' he said to Al, 'but what are you doing here? You are not a member of staff, you are not, I believe, a parent of any of the children in the school, you are not one of Her Majesty's Inspectors of Education . . .'

'Dead right so far.'

Trevor nipped in quickly, hoping a cheerful and polite introduction would ease the tension. 'Mr Wheeler, the headmaster of the school. And this is –'

'How do you do, headmaster, people call me Big Al.'

He held out a large, cheerful right hand. Wheeler touched it tentatively, as if expecting barbed wires concealed in the palm.

'Would you please leave the school grounds immediately?'

'I am a free man, Mr Wheeler. Your school belongs to the people. But I'll go anyway, 'cos I have to see Little Norm.' Al patted Trevor on the shoulder. 'See you around, Trev.' He headed towards the main gate.

'Mr Chaplin, will you ensure that undesirables do not lurk around this playground in future?'

'I'll mention it to my friends.'

Trevor watched as Mr Wheeler, cloak fluttering in the breeze, headed across the playground, shouting at kids, randomly selected.

'Are you eating, boy? You should know by now that

eating is forbidden! That's why we supply school dinners.'

His shrill commandments were lost in the babble of youthful voices.

'Pillock,' muttered Trevor.

The ripples caused by Sergeant Hobson's use of town planning regulations had lapped other shores. One of them was called Superintendent Forrest. Hobson was summoned to his office. He expected to be shouted at, and he was right.

'What's all this about Big Al?'

'I fixed him, sir.'

'Fixed him? What sort of language is that from a university graduate with first class honours?'

'I think it fairly describes what I did to him, sir. I fixed him, on the grounds that storing goods in the basement of a parish church is a breach of the town planning regulations.'

'Town planning regulations!'

This was a cue for Forrest to get up from his desk and take an irate and impatient walk around his office. He gave a stray leaf of the rubber plant a fierce back-handed slap.

'We're not in business to enforce the law, Hobson.'

'I was under the impression that –'

Forrest broke in, before Hobson could complete what seemed to him a totally legitimate observation.

'Not that sort of law. Not town planning law. They have rooms full of little grey men to do that. Little grey laws. Little grey men. Us ... we're about big grown-up law. Criminal law. Robbing and killing and maiming.'

Spoken with Forrest's Liverpool-Irish accent, the three words lost their terminal 'g' making them sound like the sparetime pursuits of a country gentleman.

He returned to his desk and sat down, a little calmer now.

'I mean, it's like nicking Rasputin for keeping a budgie in his council flat.'

He lapsed into silence and fingered through the pages of Hobson's report. His circuit of the office seemed to have consumed his immediate surplus energy.

'Just carry on with your thesis. Stop trying to nick people. Find a road and control some traffic. Protect old ladies. Or even ...' He indicated the assorted files, memo pads, telephones and heaps of paper scattered around the desk, according to a system well buried in chaos. 'Or even fill your desk, and your working hours, with meaningless ritual. It works for me, Hobson. It could work for you.'

The Hobson ripples provoked an immediate reaction from Jill Swinburne.

'Town planning regulations? I know all about town planning regulations!'

They were in the van, on their way home from school. Trevor was going to collect his toothbrush and then proceed to the flat, in accordance with the Helen of Tadcaster agreement.

'Fancy,' said Trevor, 'I've known you all these years and didn't realize you were a planning expert.'

'I am Jill Swinburne, your Conservation candidate. I am the undefeated champion where the environment's concerned. See those trees?'

They were driving past a brace of oak trees, sandwiched between a cycle shop and a redundant filling station, victim of some OPEC decision, now forgotten. Trevor looked at the trees, dutifully.

'I see those trees.'

'The corporation was going to chop them down. I saved them.'

'Wow.'

As soon as they arrived at Jill's house, she headed for the telephone, while Trevor tried to remember where he had last seen his toothbrush.

Jill could remember the town hall number and the appropriate extension to the planning department from the great battle over the oak trees, and other, even mightier campaigns.

'Extension 315, Mr Anderson please.'

She waited. That was always part of the pattern too, while cupboards were turned out and filing cabinets searched for the person you wished to speak to. She was still waiting when Trevor came down the stairs.

'I've got my toothbrush. See you in the morning.'

Jill gave him a business-like nod, indicating she had understood the message but was too busy at the moment to give it her immediate attention. He hovered in the doorway, then left the house, assuming she might send him a memo in due course.

She saw the yellow van drive away down the street and round the corner on to the main road. The people in the planning office were still looking for Mr Anderson. There were clicks on the line. It sounded as if they were looking for Mr Anderson in a packet of crisps. Then the line went dead as somebody, whether by accident, design, malice, ignorance or as a form of political protest, pressed the button on the town hall switchboard.

Jill was used to this. Saving oak trees requires great patience and understanding in the matter of telephoning the planning department. She tried again. The town hall number was engaged.

By the time she had been reconnected, extension 315

was engaged. Presumably they had found Mr Anderson and he was talking to somebody else.

Ten minutes after starting the process in the first place, she re-established a form of communication with extension 315. At that precise moment, Trevor was trudging up the stairs leading to his attic flat. He reached the top landing, stared and smiled.

A bold chalk arrow pointed up the wall towards a ledge above the door. Trevor felt along the ledge and found the key that Big Al had borrowed. He pushed the key in the lock and turned it. Then he turned the handle. The door moved no more than six inches. It felt as if a great weight were pushing against it from the other side. Trevor peered through the keyhole but saw nothing. Contrary to received wisdom, there is very little to be seen through the average keyhole. He tried the letter box.

He discovered what was preventing him from opening his front door. It looked like a gas cooker.

More or less simultaneously, Jill Swinburne made a discovery about Mr Anderson of the planning department. He had left the job a year ago. She then, rashly perhaps, asked who had taken his place. This caused uncertainty and consternation among those people by now apparently gathered around extension 315. Jill heard the muffled sounds of low-level decision-making. Then she was told that Mr Anderson had indeed been replaced, but the replacement had already gone home, since it was almost five o'clock and there had been a 'flu virus in the department.

By brandishing her track record over the oak trees and her role in the forthcoming Council by-election, she was able to wrench an official concession: an appointment the following day, at four-thirty in the afternoon, with the man who now occupied Mr Anderson's desk. He was still a man with no name. As she hung up, Jill wondered idly whether he might look like Clint Eastwood, but calculated the odds against as astronomical.

She was saddened by the news of Mr Anderson's departure. He was a man who understood the needs of the environment, and had acted as a mole in the department for preservationists and conservationists and related groups who enjoy a good cause and being a bloody nuisance to local government.

The doorbell rang as Jill was filling the kettle for a cup of tea. Trevor was outside on the step.

'Where have you been?'

'To the flat. I told you I was going. You were on the phone.'

Jill remembered. Once she was embarked on a campaign, she went into an ideological orbit and spent long periods out of the earth's regular atmosphere where people like Trevor left by the front door saying: see you in the morning.

They had walked into the living-room and sat down before Jill was sufficiently re-oriented to ask the next and obvious question.

'Why did you ring the bell? You've got a key.'

'Don't you remember? I moved out. You and Helen tossed a coin and you lost. So I'm supposed to be staying at the flat. And in the circumstances, I thought I should ring the bell. Not take anything for granted.'

Jill, fully restored to the world of emotions, feelings, clanking egos and rivalry for Trevor's affections, looked sharply at him.

'You shouldn't be here at all!'

'That's what I keep saying. I know I'm supposed to be at the flat, waiting for Helen to phone me, but there's a gas cooker against the door and a refrigerator in my bed.'

She was surprisingly warm to his request for overnight

146

accommodation, despite the gentlewoman's agreement with Helen.

'All right by me. The house seems quiet when you're not here.'

Trevor was taken off guard. Jill had betrayed the merest hint of a glimmer of a suggestion of a feeling of not quite love. By her standards, it was a clarion call from the rooftops. He got up and crossed to the settee where she was sitting, working out a firm but discreet approach to placing an arm around her shoulder. As he reached the settee, she stood up.

'Now where did I put my copy of the Town and Country Planning Act?'

Sergeant Hobson was an honest man. He believed in trust and integrity. He had never sneaked at school and never cheated in examinations. If he were to see a pin he would pick it up and hand it in at the nearest lost property office.

Now, Sergeant Hobson, BA, was confronting the ultimate challenge to his honour and to his vision of a better world. He was contemplating a step into the unknown, into uncharted territory from which the old Sergeant Hobson, BA, might never return. He was giving long, agonized and tortured consideration to becoming a bent copper.

After six hours of brooding, he reached his decision. His first step was to walk along the High Street to Boots the Chemists.

Prompt at four-thirty, Jill was in the town hall, looking for the planning department. Trevor was circling the town hall, in his van, looking for a parking meter.

It was over a year since Jill's last visit and the department had been reorganized. The man at the desk downstairs had directed her to room 5005. She walked along a fifth floor corridor that might have been designed by Kafka: 5000, 5001, 5002, 5003, 5004, 3887 . . .

She returned to the Inquiry desk on the ground floor and asked what had become of room 5005. The man behind the desk, wearing a uniform that looked as if it had been bought cheap when the Roxy cinema closed down, leafed through a large book. He concluded that room 5005 had indeed been mislaid, but suggested she go to the third floor and ask.

Jill walked along a corridor on the third floor, scanning the numbers on the doors: 3884, 3885, 3886, 5005. The system was simplicity itself once you got the hang of it. She knocked at the door, and went in.

Across a vastness of paper that presumably concealed a desk, she saw the man she had been promised: the successor to Mr Anderson. He was, at first glance, a step in the wrong direction. His name was Pitt, his age about thirty, and his ambition to cling by his fingernails to the promise of superannuation. He combined the vitality of a weak shandy with the joy of a decaying tooth.

'Mrs Swinburne, do come in. I hope you didn't have too much trouble finding us.'

'Not too much trouble. Had it been too much trouble, I would have given up completely and gone home.'

He waved a flabby, indecisive hand, inviting her to sit down.

'The trouble is, we're still unreorganized.'

'Unreorganized?'

Pitt had read a departmental leaflet about the value of open government and the citizen's right to know. He could tell Mrs Swinburne was a citizen, and come Hell or high water, she was going to know.

'The department is in the process of being reorganized, but my office is, as yet, *un*reorganized.'

'I see,' said Jill, though she didn't. She was calculating how best to deal with Mr Pitt, hovering between guile and intimidation, though the residual housewife in her felt a strong compulsion to dust him, before proceeding to questions of town planning. She settled for an opening gambit based on simple fact.

'What happened to Mr Anderson?'

'He left.'

'Why?'

'I'm sure you wouldn't expect me to tell you that, Mrs Swinburne.'

Pitt had also read a confidential departmental leaflet pointing out that despite the undoubted value of open government and the citizen's right to know, the voters should not be given information that was, in the officer's view, none of their damned business. He smiled at Jill, happy that so far he had been totally faithful to conflicting departmental leaflets. It was a neat trick, nicely executed and worth a smile. Jill was much less happy.

'Of course I expect you to tell me that! Mr Anderson was a loyal friend of conservation. He cared about the environment. He was full of good ideas.'

Pitt nodded his agreement. 'I think that might have been the problem, Mrs Swinburne.'

'You'll have to explain that.'

He leaned forward, elbows on desk, and two files slid on to the floor, unaccustomed to sudden movement of this kind. Pitt ignored them. He was concentrating on the careful middle line between departmental leaflets.

'There was a view in the department that Mr Anderson had too many ideas. That is not my view. In my position, I have no point of view.'

'Where did Mr Anderson go?'

'Australia, I think. Just one moment.'

He sat back in his chair, stared into the middle-distance,

then opened a drawer in his desk. The vibration dislodged another file. It fell gently into a waste-paper basket.

Jill checked the floor area around the desk. It was covered to a depth of six inches in files, plans and application forms. Pitt found what he was looking for. He held out a picture postcard showing blue sky and sparkling water. Jill held out a hand, to take the card from him, but he withdrew it. It was clearly highly confidential.

'Is that from Mr Anderson?'

'From Perth in Western Australia. Where he now lives.'

'And is he having a nice time?'

Jill's attempt at mild sarcasm was taken as a citizen's request for information. Pitt peered at the back of the card with the myopic intensity of a man who needs glasses but is too cowardly to go to an optician.

'He says ... the weather is very good.'

Pitt replaced the postcard in the drawer and closed it firmly, ensuring that no more vital information could escape. Then he stood up, assuming the interview was at an end.

'It's been very nice to meet you, Mrs Swinburne. I hope I have been able to clarify these matters.'

Jill remained firmly seated.

'I haven't asked you anything yet. All we've done is talk about Mr Anderson.'

'But it is almost five o'clock and we've had a 'flu bug in the department.'

'Tell me about the parish church of St Matthew. Tell me why it is an offence to store goods in the basement. Tell me about the deal you struck with Detective Sergeant Hobson.'

Her three instructions landed like successive hammer blows, driving him in stages back to the seated position.

'I'm sure you wouldn't expect me to tell you those things, Mrs Swinburne.'

'Would you prefer me to tear my clothes, scream at the top of my voice and accuse you of rape?'

It was a disreputable tactic that she was ashamed of using, but it had the value of working. Pitt stared at her, transfixed. He could recall nothing in either of the departmental leaflets about false accusations of rape.

'Just one moment, please.'

He got up from his chair and trampled through the files and drawings towards a filing cabinet.

While Pitt the Planner was delving in his filing cabinet, Trevor Chaplin was completing his eighth circuit of the town hall, in search of a place to park.

Sergeant Hobson emerged from Boots the Chemists clutching a small package. He did not notice Trevor's van. Trevor did not see Sergeant Hobson.

In the still unreorganized room 5005, Pitt outlined the prevailing gospel as it applied to church basements.

'A church is a church and a warehouse is a warehouse. You could apply for planning permission to use a church as a warehouse or even vice versa, but I doubt very much whether we would give such permission.'

'That is your point of view?'

'Bearing in mind I have no point of view, yes.'

Conducting any kind of rational debate with this man was, Jill decided, like trying to strain porridge; but she was an astute and experienced campaigner, and she spotted the Achilles heel.

'Very well, Mr Pitt. You have no point of view.'

'Correct.'

'So we are left with the question: *who* has the point of view?'

'Pardon?'

He quivered, ever so slightly. The Achilles heel became a jugular, and she went for it.

'Somebody comes into your office with a planning problem. It involves a point of view. You have no point of view. Therefore you consult the person with the point of view. Who is this person?'

Pitt was obviously disconcerted, so much so that he made a token effort at tidying his floor, picking up the files that had fallen off the desk in the course of the discussion, before murmuring: 'The chairman of the planning committee.'

'Name?'

'Councillor McAllister.'

Jill caught the exhilarating scent of a small victory. Trevor had told her of Harry's confession.

'Does he have chemists' shops and poncey restaurants and farms and a daughter called Helen who's trying to transfer a man from my bed to hers?'

Pitt made a slight movement towards his filing cabinet, as if to check, then changed his mind.

'I truly do not know the answer to that question, Mrs Swinburne. But on reflection, I believe Councillor McAllister has a brother with chemists' shops and restaurants and farms.'

Jill stood up. She had nailed the beginnings of a possible conspiracy and was a happy woman.

'Thank you, Mr Pitt. I must go now. It's well past five o'clock and there's been a 'flu virus in your department.'

Jill's euphoria at discovering the McAllister connection produced less enthusiasm from Trevor than she had expected. She had come out of the town hall just as he was feeding twenty pence into the parking meter he had found on his thirteenth circuit.

On their return home, it was her turn to prepare the food, and he made sour remarks about her vegetarian pasta. It was only when they sat in the executive through-lounge, drinking their coffee, that he rediscovered his investigative zeal.

'I get it. Helen's Daddy doesn't like Big Al stealing business from him. Helen's Daddy's brother uses his clout with the planners to push Al out of the church basement. And I end up with a refrigerator in my bed.'

'Well done, Mr Chaplin. You should be a teacher.'

'And a pound to a penny, it was the McAllisters organized the smashing up of the greenhouse.'

'And also wrecked my election meeting.'

'It's great, isn't it? Let's crack another bottle of Frascati.'

Trevor was overtaken by a bout of decisiveness and, without waiting for a second opinion from Jill, went to the kitchen for more wine.

As he filled their glasses he asked: 'What are we going to do now, Butch?'

'Easy,' said Jill. 'When Helen makes contact with you, all you have to do is get yourself invited round to her place, chat up Daddy, and see what the Hell he's up to.'

'Easy? Is that easy?'

'Simple,' said Jill. 'All you need is an invitation to Sunday lunch.'

'I can't do that! If I say to her: excuse me, Helen, can I come to lunch on Sunday, I'd like to have a serious talk with your father ... he's bound to think ...'

Jill completed the dreadful thought. 'Ham salads. Wedding bells.'

'Right.'

'I give you fair warning, Mr Chaplin. If you get engaged to that girl, I shall insist you move into the spare room.'

Before they could pursue the moral implications any further, the doorbell rang.

'Jehovah's Witnesses?' said Trevor.

'Double-glazing,' said Jill.

'Ten pence in the Oxfam box for the winner.'

It was a traditional arrangement they had when trying to guess who was at the door. Jill went into the hallway to answer it while Trevor topped up the glasses. Jill returned with Helen, who seemed surprised and a little put out at Trevor's presence.

'Hello, Helen.'

'Hello, Trevor.'

'Little drop of Frascati?'

'No, thank you.'

Helen was persuaded to sit down. That was as much hospitality as she was prepared to accept.

'I didn't expect to find you here, Trevor.'

'Who did you expect?'

He had drunk three-quarters of a bottle of wine and was feeling marginally skittish, as was Jill. Helen had drunk nothing and was isolated as only the stone-cold sober can be.

'I telephoned your flat last night. There was no reply. I telephoned again this evening. There was still no reply. I went round to the flat. You were not there.'

'I can't get in. There's a refrigerator in my bed.'

'You know about that?'

'Of course I do. It's my bed.'

Helen relaxed and owned up.

'When I went to the flat and there was no reply, I looked through the letter box. I saw the refrigerator in your bed.'

'I'm looking after it for a friend.'

'Thank you, I will have a glass of wine.'

Jill poured the wine on the troubled waters, hoping it would ease the tension but not totally. Helen sipped from her glass and smiled for the first time since her arrival.

'I've actually come with an invitation.'

'For both of us?' asked Jill.

'For Trevor,' said Helen, smartly.

'Great.'

'My parents wondered if you'd like to come to lunch on Sunday. Daddy would love to see you again.'

Jill and Trevor knew they ought not to laugh. They knew it was extremely ill-mannered to giggle when the other person in the room could not understand the joke. They knew they would feel ashamed of themselves if they did laugh. And they tried, genuinely and sincerely, to control themselves. They failed.

Helen gaped at their hysterics, baffled.

'Have I said something funny?'

'No,' said Jill, laughing.

'No,' emphasized Trevor, also laughing.

'I don't understand,' said Helen.

'I'll explain over lunch on Sunday.'

This offer, which might theoretically have had a calming effect, only zapped up the hysteria several decibels. There were tears in Jill's eyes, and Trevor was on the brink of having to stuff a handkerchief in his mouth, in a quest for self-control.

The doorbell came to the rescue.

'Double-glazing?' said Trevor.

'Jehovah's Witnesses,' said Jill.

'Ten pence in the Oxfam box.'

'What's all that about?' asked Helen, as Jill went to answer the door.

'The doorbell,' replied Trevor.

While Jill was in the hallway, Helen moved quickly across the room and sat beside Trevor on the settee, in the warm spot Jill had vacated. She spoke quickly and urgently: 'Trevor. I want you to know that I'm glad she called heads and lost. I know it was a silly game at the time but I've been thinking about it ever since and I'm glad I won. It isn't a silly game to me.'

She was very close to him, expecting an answer.

'Er ...' was the best he could manage.

'Come on, Trevor, I've opened my heart to you. I'm entitled to a better response than er ...'

He was in a tricky spot and they both knew it. Even to look directly into her eyes while saying nothing could well be interpreted as a gesture of love everlasting. His reply had been truthful and sincere. The music from his heart was precisely that: er ...

'Well, Trevor?'

He smiled and his eyes suddenly shone brightly.

'Oh look, a policeman!' he said.

Jill had returned, accompanied by Sergeant Hobson, who, like Helen, was immediately aware of the giggling in the atmosphere. Jill introduced him with an almost cavalier flourish.

'Sergeant Hobson, our neighbourhood CID man ... Helen of Tadcaster, my rival in love. That's the story so far. Now read on.'

She sat down and poured herself some more wine, while Hobson nodded politely at Helen.

'Good evening ...' Then he turned towards Trevor: '... but it's really Mr Chaplin I want to see.'

'Well, here I am. Have a good look,' said Trevor. He and Jill sniggered again, but more quietly this time.

'I need your assistance with some inquiries I am making, Mr Chaplin.'

He was irritated by their laughter. It was not a proper response to a well spoken request from a plain-clothes detective.

'Do you find that funny, Mrs Swinburne?'

'Not particularly. The one that really makes me laugh

is when somebody says: "But there's one thing I still don't understand, inspector."'

She saw that Hobson's face carried the head-back joviality of a well formed glacier, and calculated a partial apology was in order.

'Forgive me, officer, but we've been drinking Italian wine.'

'Does it always have this effect?'

'At the very least,' said Jill.

'Would you like some?' asked Trevor, waving the bottle politely in Hobson's direction, who ignored the invitation.

'Mr Chaplin. I have reason to believe there is stolen property at your flat. I would like you to accompany me there, so that we might check the situation.'

'There's a refrigerator in his bed,' said Helen, not sure which side she was on.

'I know,' replied Hobson.

'Did you look through the letter-box too?' asked Helen, deciding that she was not on Hobson's side. He had after all disturbed a very tender moment.

'Yes, I did, since you ask. Are you coming, Mr Chaplin?'

Trevor got up, and realized the wine had taken effect, as his instinctive shrug almost threw him off balance.

'We'd better go in your car, I've been drinking.'

'I'll get your jacket,' said Jill. It was not like her to run after him in this way, but it was a calculated ploy that enabled her to slip a copy of *Citizen's Guide If Busted* into the pocket.

The two women watched as Hobson's car drove away, Helen more anxiously than Jill.

'Does this happen often?'

'The police? Stuff like that?'

'Yes.'

'Occasionally. He's been questioned now and again. Loitering and prowling. That class of offence. Alleged offence, I should say. He's never been tried and convicted. Stolen property, that's new. Come on, Helen, help me finish this wine.'

Helen drank uneasily, wondering if it had been a good toss to win.

It took the combined force of Trevor and Hobson to push the door of the flat open far enough to permit entry. Once inside, Trevor switched the light on and the two of them inspected the array of cookers, refrigerators, wheelbarrows and hedge trimmers crammed into the available space.

There was another large, chalked arrow on the wall, pointing at a bunch of receipts and invoices, clipped together. Trevor picked these up. They were the evidence that all the property was legitimate and thoroughly clean in every respect.

Hobson checked each item in turn, while Trevor presented him with the appropriate invoice.

'Microwave oven.'

'Check.'

'Record player.'

'Check.'

'Hair dryer.'

'Check.'

'Electric toothbrush.'

'Pardon?'

There was no reference in any of the documents to an electric toothbrush. Hobson waited until Trevor had leafed through the wad of papers twice, then, with a cool certainty that he had been working on all day, murmured: 'You are well and truly nicked, my old son.'

At the police station, Trevor was left in an interview room for a few minutes while Hobson pretended to be making phone calls in his office. He had no phone calls to make, but Joe and Ben had advised him that leaving a suspect alone for five minutes before an interview was a great way to focus his mind and dredge the guilt to the surface. Trevor used the time to read the copy of *Citizen's Guide If Busted*. He was well prepared when Hobson returned.

'Now, Mr Chaplin –'

'You haven't cautioned me.'

'Pardon?'

'You haven't cautioned me. Page three in the book. You're supposed to say all that about anything I say will be taken down and used in evidence.'

'I will administer the caution in my own good time, Mr Chaplin.'

Trevor persisted: 'Unless you caution me, I'm not under arrest, in which case I must be here voluntarily, in which case I'd rather go home, which is my right, see page five. Good night, Mr Hobson.'

He got up and walked across to the door. Hobson grabbed him by the arm.

'Trevor Chaplin, I am arresting you for being in possession of stolen property. Anything you say may be taken down and used in evidence against you.'

'That's better,' said Trevor, returning peacefully to his seat.

'Good. Now, Mr Chaplin –'

'Can I make my phone call now? I am entitled to make one phone call, see page seven.'

He pushed the booklet across the table, open at page seven. Hobson ignored it. There was a telephone on the desk.

'Who do you want to ring? Your lawyer?'

Trevor shook his head. He knew better people than lawyers.

*

Jill answered the telephone.

'Trevor! Where are you? The 87th precinct? On what charge? An electric toothbrush!'

After hanging up, she could not decide whether it was funny or not. She outlined the plot to Helen. Trevor had been charged with being in possession of a stolen electric toothbrush.

'What does he want?' asked Helen.

'Help,' said Jill.

Helen stood up and crossed to the phone. A glass of Frascati and the urge to protect the innocent combined to give a jaunty defiance to her manner.

'I can help,' she said confidently, picking up the receiver.

'You?' said Jill, suddenly usurped from her role as fighter for rights, defender of the poor and dispossessed.

'Well, I did win the toss.'

Helen dialled a number that she knew better than any in the massed directories of the United Kingdom. Daddy answered.

Sergeant Hobson was sceptical about the phone call to Jill.

'Mrs Swinburne leaping into action on your behalf, is she?'

'You can expect a strongly-worded petition within the next ten days.'

Trevor had no idea what Jill would do. He had a vague expectation that a posse, led by Big Al on a white horse, might break the door down and carry him away across the Lancashire border.

Hobson, certain that his suspect had exhausted the possibilities of the *Citizen's Guide*, felt he had regained the initiative. His immediate objective was a written statement.

'Now, Mr Chaplin –'

'I'd like to make a written statement.'

Their needs apparently coincided. Hobson smiled.

'It is your legal right so to do.'

He slid a sheet of paper across the desk.

'Is it all right if I use my own pen?' asked Trevor. Hobson nodded his official assent.

Hobson watched as Trevor wrote, in large capital letters, perfected on blackboards down the long years of school-teaching: I DO NOT POSSESS AN ELECTRIC TOOTHBRUSH. At the bottom of the page he signed his name: Trevor Chaplin.

'That's not a statement!'

'Of course it's a statement. It's true. I do not possess an electric toothbrush.'

Hobson grabbed the statement and tore it up.

'That's vital evidence,' said Trevor. 'What's more, it's the only statement you'll get out of me. Take me to my cell. I'd like an early morning call about eight.'

Trevor stood up again, and headed for the door.

'Stay where you are, Mr Chaplin!' said Hobson.

The door opened and was filled by the considerable bulk of Superintendent Forrest, wearing evening dress, and looking equal parts a 1930s bandleader and a 1980s bouncer. He also wore an expression of severely contained venom.

'Go home, son,' he said to Trevor.

'But I'm under arrest.'

'Your arrest is a figment of Sergeant Hobson's imagination. Like many other things.'

He put a friendly arm around Trevor's shoulder. It felt like the beginning of a wrestling throw.

'You're a lucky lad. You have friends of power and influence.'

'Have I?' It was news to Trevor.

'Indeed you have. Whereas Sergeant Hobson has no friends of power and influence.'

It was clear to all three that a gale-force bollocking was

heading towards Hobson, targeted right between the eyes.

'Hard luck, sergeant,' said Trevor. 'Good night all.'

Forrest waited until Trevor was decently along the corridor before uncorking his indignation.

'Do you know why sir is dressed like an overweight penguin? Because sir was attending an official dinner with lord mayors and chief constables and bishops. Medal ribbons everywhere. The Blue Nun flowing like water. And sir was dragged away from this municipal bacchanalia by an urgent phone call to say that you had been trying to fit somebody up with an electric toothbrush!'

Forrest sat down at the table in the chair previously occupied by Trevor. He unfastened his bow-tie and drank deeply and gratefully from a hipflask. Refreshed, the diatribe continued: 'On the one hand, I am deeply grateful, because the music was about to start, and I was about to be forced to dance with my wife. On the other hand, I am so weary of you, Sergeant Hobson, oh so weary. I mean to say, an electric toothbrush.'

The superintendent slumped forward on the table. Hobson could not decide whether he was drunk or sleeping. Booze or doze? Perhaps boze was the appropriate word? Hobson pulled himself together. He was becoming as crazy as those around him.

The decent humanitarian reaction was to give black coffee to Mr Forrest. He asked the desk constable to see to it as he left the building.

Trevor wore his suit on Sunday. He had bought it for his sister's wedding and loathed it. He also hated the shirt and tie that a sharp-talking salesman had promised him would make a perfect match. Trevor Chaplin was a jeans and tee-shirt man. Sartorial elegance was for other people.

Nonetheless, Helen was impressed as she met him in the

extensive gravel drive that spread itself evenly and neatly in front of the McAllister house. The yellow van sat incongruously among the Mercs, like a plastic gnome in the Hanging Gardens of Babylon.

'You look very smart, Trevor,' said Helen, as she took him by the hand and led him through a wrought-iron gate into a garden that stretched as far as the eye could see. 'Daddy's sitting by the pool.'

'I thought he might be,' said Trevor. The house and grounds made Sandringham look like a highly-mortgaged semi. In the middle distance, Trevor glimpsed a flash of bright blue which, as he came closer, turned out to be a kidney-shaped swimming pool. Beside it was a table, chairs, a drinks cabinet, and Helen's Daddy, relaxing with a Glenfiddich and the *News Of The World*. He may have been taken rich but had not betrayed his humble roots.

'Trevor!' said McAllister, standing up, putting down his newspaper and holding out a large fleshy hand. 'Welcome to –'

'Your humble abode?' suggested Trevor, with a backward glance at the Yorkshireman's castle.

'Still got the sense of humour. I like a sense of humour in a man. Sit down, Trevor.'

It was a hot day. McAllister wore Bermuda shorts and a loose flapping multi-coloured shirt designed to conceal the belly that runneth over. Trevor and Helen sat down. Trevor accepted a drink of Glenfiddich. He had once priced it in an off-licence. It was worth every penny.

'Do you like the house?' asked McAllister.

'Yes,' said Trevor, 'it's very ... homely.'

'And it is done by not making waves.'

There was nothing homely in the fat man's statement about the order of things. Trevor realized what he had half-suspected. The summons to Sunday lunch included a compulsory shot across the bows.

'Daddy likes to be cryptic,' said Helen, who had different plans for the day.

'Too cryptic for me,' said Trevor.

'Electric toothbrush.'

McAllister's words fell on the steam heat of the day like a blacksmith's hammer on an anvil. Trevor decided to play innocent. It seemed reasonable, since he was innocent.

'Did you do that?'

McAllister nodded. 'And I think you should say thank you, Trevor.'

'Thank you, Mr McAllister. I wonder ...' Trevor hesitated; then, remembering Jill's briefing before he had left the house, headed directly for the essential information: '... how did you do it?'

Like most self-made men, McAllister enjoyed glorying in his own achievements. 'Simple. Helen phoned me. I phoned my brother ...'

'Councillor McAllister?' asked Trevor, anxious to have the story crystal clear.

'Yes. He's on the Police Authority. What we used to call the watch committee when I was a lad. And he had a word with a friend in high places.'

'Superintendent Forrest?'

'That's right. We're all golfing chums. You know the sort of thing.'

Trevor did not know the sort of thing intimately but was beginning to get the hang of it.

'Any road,' said McAllister, asserting his roots again, 'that's not the only thing I want to talk to you about. Helen ...'

He looked at his daughter in a way that conveyed the simple message: this is men's talk, clear off. Helen stood up, dutifully, and set off towards the house.

'Where are you going?' asked Trevor.

'To help with the lunch.'

'Also this only concerns you and me,' said McAllister.

'Does it concern Helen?' asked Trevor.

'Yes.'

'If it concerns Helen, how can it only concern me and you?' said Trevor.

'Women's Lib time is it?' McAllister spat out the words. 'Did you catch it from that woman you're living with?'

The phrase startled Trevor. He had certainly never thought of Jill as the woman he was living with. She was Jill, and he sometimes stayed at her house. They laughed and argued and had lots of fun. They drove each other mad and kept each other sane. To call her the woman he was living with made her sound scarlet and sinful.

'That, Mr McAllister, is the daftest thing I've heard for years.'

It was not the most tactful of remarks. McAllister exploded, as only the nouveau riche can when insulted by the lower orders who haven't yet cracked the system.

'All right, Trevor, try this for daftness. If you and Helen are going to get together again, and I would welcome that, make no mistake, there are certain things you have to do. You move out of that woman's house and go back to your flat immediately. In addition, you stop mixing with un-desirables who disturb the equilibrium that pays for this house and this swimming pool.'

'Do you mean Big Al?'

'I'm naming no names. I'm just saying get rid of your fancy woman and get rid of your funny friends and ...' He smiled a car-salesman smile. '... and come and have some lunch.'

'Bollocks,' said Trevor.

As Trevor walked across the grounds in the direction of

the McAllister car park, Helen pursued him, on the brink
of tears.

'Don't go, Trevor, he doesn't mean it, he's an old softy
really.'

'He can afford to be. It's time you liberated yourself,
Helen. Unless you're going to live off his pieces of silver
for the rest of your life.'

'You've changed.'

Trevor opened the door of his van.

'This is the new dynamic Trevor Chaplin. Nobody wins
me on the toss of a coin. It might have worked in old money
but . . .'

Helen grabbed at his arm as he was climbing into the
van.

'Don't go. My mother was so keen to see you again. And
she was up half the night with her stroganoff.'

'There you go,' he said, 'what use is money if you haven't
got good health.'

As Trevor drove off along the gravel drive that curved
its way around a gentle hillside towards the nearest
motorway, he wound his window down and shouted at the
top of his voice: 'Goodbye for ever!' He had no idea
whether Helen heard, but he was sure she had grasped the
message. On the way to Jill's house he stopped at an Indian
takeaway and bought a chicken vindaloo. He found her in
the tiny back garden, delving in dusty box files. He peeled
away the foil cover from his meal.

'You can't beat a proper Sunday dinner,' he said.

It was the first time Trevor Chaplin had taken part in an
assignation at level four of the multi-storey car park behind
the bus station. It was Jill's idea.

While he had been at the McAllister house, asserting
the rights of women, flaunting the new-style, emancipated

Chaplin image, Jill had sat in her little garden, eating natural yoghurt and working through files, ancient and modern, related to conservation issues and civil liberties cases that she had fought. Sometimes she had won, sometimes she had lost, and sometimes it had gone to extra time and penalties. The pattern that repeated was the involvement of three men: Superintendent Forrest and the brothers McAllister.

Jill had a finely-tuned sense of justice and she knew the evidence was flimsy. Properly presented in court, it might result in a small fine and a public warning. But there was powerful circumstantial evidence that the three men had been involved, hip-deep, in the manipulation of planning regulations and the discreet persecution of radical groups with curious ideas and aspirations like peace and the survival of the human species.

Knowing that the evidence of her files was flimsy, she had decided a touch of the theatrical might help the cause. Simply delivering her evidence to Hobson's office, or having him collect from the house, would make it seem as feeble as it undoubtedly was. An assignation in a suitably sinister location would add drama to the handover, and substance to the prosecution case.

After long discussions with Trevor, level four at the multi-storey car park emerged as the natural contender. Multi-storey car parks looked good in thriller movies and, as Trevor pointed out, you could park there for nothing on a Sunday evening. Jill had telephoned Sergeant Hobson, stating time and place, dropping the name Forrest, and hoping for the best. Hobson had agreed.

Level four was deserted. Trevor and Jill sat in the van, gazing at the bleak, deserted parking bays.

'This is ludicrous,' said Trevor.

'I know.'

At the far end of level four, Hobson's car drove slowly

into view. He parked, switched off the engine and flashed his headlights twice. That had been Trevor's idea. He flashed the van's headlights twice in reply.

Jill climbed out of the van. Hobson climbed out of the car. They walked slowly towards each other. Jill carried the box file in which she had crammed all her available evidence. Trevor watched through his windscreen. The two figures approaching each other reminded him of a film. Was it *High Noon*?

The two of them met.

'Is that the file?'

'Yes.' Jill handed it over with the warning: 'But if challenged, I will deny seeing you here this evening.'

'I understand, Mrs Swinburne. Thank you.'

He had been brought up to say thank you. He grasped the file carefully, seeing a vision of Forrest behind bars, curiously enough wearing an arrowed uniform of the sort worn by convicts in children's comics.

Hobson turned to go back to his car, then hesitated.

'Mrs Swinburne.'

'Sergeant Hobson?'

'Do you ever go to the pictures?'

'Yes, but I'm washing my hair tonight, ready for the by-election.'

Hobson smiled, a genuine smile from the heart. Jill had never never seen such a thing on his face before.

'I wasn't asking for a date,' he said, 'I was simply going to observe ... I think this could be the beginning of a beautiful friendship.'

Six

There were forty-eight hours to go before polling day in the Council by-election at Northfield Central (South). Jill's campaign was reaching its second peak, the first having been the meeting in the Institute, cancelled owing to her non-existent illness.

The second high point was drawing a larger crowd. Two small children and a local skateboarder were gathered around Trevor's van, as he attached a loudspeaker to its roof, and an assortment of wires and a microphone to the dashboard. The first time he tested it, it gave off a high-pitched whine and a blue flash that frightened the small children away. The second time he tested it, he announced to the neighbourhood: 'We are on the brink of a new era if only . . .'

Then the circuit went dead. Jill came out of the house carrying some placards for the van. Trevor was lying flat on his back across the front seat attempting subtleties with insulating tape.

'What was that you said, Mr Chaplin?'

'We are on the brink of a new era if only.'

'If only what?'

'If only I can get the bloody thing to work.'

Jill left him to grapple with the electronics while she attached placards on either side of the van reading: VOTE JILL SWINBURNE AND SAVE THE PLANET EARTH. The skateboarder, already a little bored, decided this was too modest a manifesto to provide many laughs and zoomed off down the road.

There was a burst of heavy breathing over the loud-speaker, followed by a triplet of puffing sounds, like a vintage steam loco clearing its throat. Jill walked around the van to find Trevor in the driving seat, microphone in hand.

'Testing,' he said.

'Go on, then. I'll stand out here and listen.'

He tweaked the volume control and over a half-mile radius the electorate was able to hear: 'My friends. Vote for Jill Swinburne. A vote for Swinburne is a vote for the planet Earth. What's more, she's terrific in bed.'

The electorate, if it was listening, might also have heard: 'Give me that thing, you stupid pillock! How do you switch it off?'

The neighbourhood resumed its normal mid-evening serenity. The only significant sounds were a local problem teenager tuning up his Honda, the swish of a bank manager practising golf swings in his garden, the occasional whine of a well bred dog, and the title music of *Coronation Street* coming from a thousand homes.

Trevor and Jill stared at the dashboard and the complicated assembly of wires dangling thereunder.

'You probably lost me the election, saying that.'

'Getaway,' said Trevor, 'I might have won you the election.'

He was a little short on political passion, but loved gadgetry. He picked up the microphone.

'Can we drive about for a bit, saying, "Vote for Swinburne"?'

'Not until Thursday.'

He shrugged and made a bad job of concealing his disappointment as Jill climbed out of the van.

'Where did Al get all this gear from anyway?' he called after her.

'His brother.'

Deep in his cloistered seclusion at the police station, Sergeant Hobson was whispering into a microphone.

'It would appear that my investigations into subjects A, B and C have led me to apparent corruption at a very high level within my own organization.'

Open on the desk in front of him was the file handed over by Jill at level four in the multi-storey car park. He looked around at the empty office, to be sure he was alone, before continuing: 'Subject F. Superintendent Forrest.'

He stopped the tape. He still found it difficult to accept the reality of Forrest's guilt. The man was rough and abusive, given to bullying, intimidation and foul-mouthed obscenities. He told crude jokes that were racist, sexist and fascist, for preference all three simultaneously. He drank throughout the working day, fell asleep at his desk at regular intervals and was, by Hobson's analysis, subject to occasional bouts of amiable, clinical insanity. All these qualities added up to a lack of professionalism – but full-blooded, twenty-four carat corruption? He decided to make an informal check.

He double-locked the tapes in a drawer and walked along the corridor to the reception area. Most evenings after eight o'clock Joe and Ben could be found leaning on the counter, pretending it was a bar. Tonight they were rehearsing for a late-night surveillance at a city centre club. Their declared aim was to keep an eye open for drug smugglers and white slavers. Their joint private intention was to get smashed on expenses.

They smiled as they spotted Hobson approaching, anticipating a little spot of homely fun.

'Good evening, sir,' said Joe. 'Can we be of any assistance?'

'I think perhaps you can,' Hobson replied, quietly. He looked around for concealed microphones and hidden cameras. There should have been hidden cameras. The building was scheduled to have them, for security purposes, but there was a two-year hold-up in delivery on the model selected. Joe and Ben picked up on his apprehension and made a great production number out of looking over their shoulders, before the three of them gathered together in a huddle around the counter.

'Supposing it came to your attention,' murmured Hobson, 'that a senior police officer in this division was guilty of corruption?'

'So what's new?' asked Joe.

'Sounds like Mr Forrest,' said Ben.

'I am not naming names!' said Hobson, firmly.

'But it's bound to be Mr Forrest,' Ben insisted. 'It's a well known fact. He's as bent as a nine-bob note.'

Joe confirmed the thesis. 'That's why we like him.'

Hobson refused to indict Forrest. He made it clear he was asking for simple and honest advice, man to man, detective to detective. He wondered about friend to friend, but decided against pushing his luck that far.

Joe was predictably helpful and practical.

'You've got a choice, sergeant. Plan A. Bundle up the evidence, tie it up in pink ribbon, take it to the chief constable. We gather the chief constable is an honest man.'

'He's done very well, considering,' said Ben.

'Plan B. Parcel up your evidence, tie it up in pink ribbon, take it to Mr Forrest.'

'It isn't Mr Forrest!' said Hobson, but Joe ignored him.

'Take it to Mr Forrest and get him to cut you in. Demand your share of the action as the price of silence.'

'Grab a seat on the board,' added Ben, in case Hobson was not clear about the method of procedure.

Hobson was extremely clear in his mind about the suggestion, and was outraged: 'That's a disgusting suggestion!'

Ben took up the running. Like his partner, he was nosing out exciting possibilities.

'OK then, how about Plan C? We could all three go to Mr Forrest, and all three share the benefit of his corruption. One for all, all for one.'

'Good film, that,' said Joe.

Before Hobson could express his horror at Plan C, the other two fell silent and sprang into a near approximation of alertness and devotion to duty. Hobson turned to see Superintendent Forrest entering through the swing doors.

'Evening, lads. Evening, Hobson,' he said, crossing to the counter. He seemed relatively sober, bearing in mind the lateness of the evening.

'Busy, are we?'

'We were just having a short discussion with Sergeant Hobson about community policing,' said Ben, handing the baton to Joe who continued, with a fluency that was eloquent testimony to their long years on the beat together: 'Prior to an urgent, all-night surveillance at the Storyville-a-Go-Go night club, sir.'

Forrest seemed happy enough with the reply. He was resigned to the fact that late-night discotheques and drinking clubs were the closest the modern world could offer to the Liverpool backstreets of his own salad days. The action had moved indoors, where it was warm. It was a pity, but he could do nothing about it. He turned to Hobson.

'And what about you? When are you planning to catch your first real villain?'

'I hope before the week is out,' replied Hobson, standing

smartly to attention and taking the chance on direct eye contact with Forrest.

Joe and Ben were impressed, despite their principled prejudice against graduate policemen, and personal prejudice against Hobson. They watched in silence as Hobson returned to his office, and waited for an appropriate one-liner from Forrest. Instead, he too seemed subdued and a little wary.

'What do you think of him?' he asked the lads.

'Compared with what?' said Joe and Ben in unison.

They had come this far unscathed by hedging their bets where senior officers were concerned and they weren't going to stop now.

Trevor's van, surmounted by its loudspeaker and bedecked with election slogans about Jill Swinburne and her plans for the planet Earth, created a deal of excitement in the school playground next morning. Mr Wheeler was less impressed and intercepted Jill and Trevor on their way into school with a profound question.

'Would you care to tell me how you see your duty and responsibility as teachers?'

It was a tough one, before nine o'clock in the morning, but Trevor did his best: 'Fill the kids with O-levels and A-levels so they know how to read a UB40?'

It was the wrong answer.

'We are here to provide a balanced education, Mrs Swinburne. The key word is balance. Which does not mean political subversion! If you read the Education Act you will find it is made abundantly clear. Teachers must not impose their political views on the children. Teachers must have no convictions whatsoever!'

'Isn't that rather difficult?' protested Jill. 'How can we vote at elections if we have no convictions?'

'Convictions must be kept secret. It is the only decent way to behave. Secrecy. But this kind of thing . . .' He flung out an arm, and an expanse of black, academic gown, in the direction of the van: '. . . contaminates the children.'

Trevor sprang loyally to Jill's defence.

'I don't think anybody's been contaminated. Mrs Swinburne's been campaigning for weeks and nobody's taken any notice at all so far.'

Neither Jill nor Mr Wheeler was thrilled with this assessment of her efforts. The headmaster now flung out his right arm towards an upper-floor window of the school.

'If nobody has been contaminated, how do you explain *that*?'

They looked up. Outside the windows of Jill's classroom a series of banners fluttered proudly in the breeze. They bore a diverse collection of statements including VOTE FOR MRS SWINBURNE, EARTH RULES OK?, JILL IS BRILL, POWER TO THE FLOWERS and MRS S FOR QUEEN. There might have been some doctrinal confusion, but there was no mistaking the loyalty and passion.

'Contamination, Mrs Swinburne, contamination!'

'I imagine it's an Art project,' said Jill.

'I shall be seeing the chairman of the school governors tomorrow, and I shall inform him of the situation.'

'The chairman of the governors? Isn't that Councillor McAllister?' Jill mused.

'It is,' confirmed Mr Wheeler. 'He is a very good friend of the school, and has the decency to keep his convictions secret.'

Jill wondered whether the McAllister convictions were previous rather than political. It might explain his reticence.

'That's a coincidence,' said Trevor, startling the other two, who were unaware of any coincidences close at hand.

'What is, Mr Chaplin?' snapped the headmaster.

'You talking about Councillor McAllister, and here comes a police car,' said Trevor, nodding across the playground, where Sergeant Hobson's car was nosing its way between the late arrivals, in practice virtually every student and teacher attending San Quentin High.

Wheeler greeted the young detective with his customary crawling subservience.

'Good morning, sergeant. How can we be of service?'

'Thank you, headmaster, but I need to speak to Mrs Swinburne concerning a major inquiry.'

Hobson stood, clean-shaven, blue eyes shining with the intensity of a man destined to clean up the town. Wheeler read the message loud and clear. He also read the footnote saying it was none of his business and would he please push off.

'School begins in five minutes,' he said, his face revealing the sulkiness of the betrayed academic.

'This will take two minutes,' chimed Hobson, with a hint of a bow. He could charm when necessary. They taught it at his minor public school when it was too wet for games.

Wheeler pushed his way through the assembly of kids into school, hurling words at individuals chosen arbitrarily from the mob: 'Haircut! ... Chewing! ... Handkerchief!'

Hobson wiped away the charm and replaced it with a brand of tight-lipped urgency that reminded Trevor of long-ago British war films starring Jack Hawkins.

'Tonight,' he said, 'multi-storey car park, level four.'

'Why?' asked Jill.

'Thanks to your initiative, I am now involved in a major investigation. But I need to talk to you. In private. Level four. Seven o'clock.'

'If it's as major as all that, shouldn't we make it level five?' Trevor suggested.

'Shuttup,' said Jill.

Hobson returned to his car and drove away.

'Are we crazy or is he?' asked Jill.

'I should think so,' said Trevor, as the siren sounded for lessons.

'Someone has blundered' was Jill's summary of their dilemma, when, at seven o'clock in the evening, they arrived at level four in the multi-storey car park, to find it crammed to overflowing. The entire philosophy of a secret assignation in a deserted car park collapses in ruins if the place is packed tight with Sierras, Volvos and Fiats.

'You can't trust people,' said Trevor. 'Fancy leaving cars in a car park.'

He completed four circuits of level four in a fruitless search for an empty bay, before a squealing of brakes at a blind corner indicated that Sergeant Hobson had found them.

The police car and the van skidded slowly to a halt, inches separating them. They stood side by side, blocking the routes in and out of the car park, but convenient for Hobson and Jill: by winding down their respective windows, they were able to have confidential discussions without the bother of getting out or the phoney melodrama of slow approaches on foot, *High Noon* style.

'Mrs Swinburne ... I need more files.'

'Files?'

'You gave me a file, implicating the McAllister brothers and Superintendent Forrest in high level corruption. I must have more evidence. I need more files if I'm to nail them.'

'He needs nail files,' muttered Trevor, to nobody except himself.

Jill wanted to help but explained the difficulty of her position: 'I'm busy saving the planet Earth this week, and I gave you all the information I could.'

'Do you know anybody who might help?'

'Mr Anderson.'

'Mr Anderson?'

'He used to work in the planning department at the town hall.'

'Used to?'

'He moved to Perth, Australia.'

'I bet Big Al could get some files,' said Trevor, again to nobody except himself, though he reckoned this a more constructive suggestion than his earlier one.

After van and car had extricated themselves from level four, Trevor drove immediately to the Tolpuddle Street allotments. They found Big Al in his office, wedged between a chest of drawers and a half-size snooker table, trimming the claws on a rabbit.

'Have you still got storage problems?' asked Trevor.

'No, Little Norm is giving it urgent attention, even as we speak.'

'What is he doing?'

'I told him to sit at home and worry about it. So he is. What can I do for you? Your claws need trimming, do they?'

Jill outlined the case for the prosecution and persecution of the McAllisters and Forrest: the bribery and corruption that had taken place, all of it part of a massive conspiracy against the common people. 'But we need more hard evidence,' she said.

'More files,' suggested Trevor, who remembered Big Al's ready supply of files.

Al tenderly placed the rabbit in a hutch, then picked his way past cardboard boxes and packing cases to the corner where his filing cabinet was buried deep. He emerged after a scuffle holding a dozen or so empty files.

'There we are. We've just got to fill them with hard evidence. Does it have to be true, this evidence?'

'It would be quite nice, don't you think?' said Jill.

Al considered the question.

'I wonder. If we're saying these three men are bent, then does it matter if the evidence that convicts them is bent as well? It's poetic justice, in a way, isn't it? He that wrecketh a greenhouse doth collecteth all that cometh to him. The vicar told me that, unless I invented it.'

Jill assured him that anything he could do to help the cause of justice would be appreciated but speaking personally, in this by-election week, she would prefer approximate truth to approximate lies. Al half-listened. He was already making plans for a busy day on the morrow.

'Affidavits. That's what we need. Affidavits. I'll get Little Norm at it, early doors.'

'Then pass it all on to Sergeant Hobson.'

'As you say, Mrs Swinburne. The man's been trying to nick me for the last fortnight, so I owe him a favour.'

Trevor lost his grip on Al's logic.

'Pardon?'

'Turn the other cheek. Do good to them that speak all manner of evil against you, falsely. It's a basic tenet of Christianity.'

'Did the vicar tell you that, too?' asked Jill.

'No, flower. It's part of the nineteenth-century nonconformist ethic that I inherited and rejected. I prefer football really.'

Following his appointment with the yellow van at the car park, Hobson called in a downtown eating-house, a one-time bank converted into a pasta joint with Neapolitan muzak and walls painted in primary colours. He ate a pizza and drank a glass of house white. The wine was warmer than the pizza, but under the terms of the menu, five pence of his bill would go to keeping Venice intact. It gave him a nice dry feeling inside.

Around nine o'clock, he drove back to the police station. He felt the need to communicate with his tape recorder and delve a little into the accumulated knowledge of the computer. So deeply embedded was he in his investigative brooding, he did not see the car following him. It was a Jaguar, driven by a man wearing dark glasses, even though it was well past sundown.

He pushed his way through the swing doors at the station. The constable at the desk ignored him, according to the now established pattern. Joe and Ben were carrying out an urgent surveillance at the dog-track, but as he walked through the deserted squad office he could see where they had been. The sign on his door had been re-drafted yet again to read: LORD HOBSON, BA.

He opened the door and went into his office. Superintendent Forrest sat at his desk, surrounded by cassettes.

'Evening, Hobson.'

'Evening, sir.'

'Come in for a spot of overtime on your thesis, have you?'

'I try not to let it interfere with my normal duties, sir.'

Forrest stood up, indicating Hobson should take his rightful place at his own desk.

'I expect you think sir has been going through your desk and cupboards, nosing around in your personal possessions.'

It was obvious that Forrest had been doing precisely that. Hobson, who knew his way around his own tape recorder, also guessed that he had been trying, in vain, to play the cassettes. Several of the buttons were in the 'down' position, but the superintendent had omitted to plug the machine in at the mains and, without electricity, it lost most of its magical powers.

Hobson buried all his unworthy thoughts behind a strictly formal response: 'I assume it's a routine security check, sir.'

'What's on these?' Forrest shuffled the tapes around on the desk, as if preparing to play a game of dominoes.

'They shouldn't really be here, sir, they're personal.'

'Personal?' Forrest smelt not one, but an entire plague of rats, all with first class honours degrees.

'Would you like to hear one?' said Hobson.

'Go on.'

Hobson selected a tape, apparently at random. He bent down, and plugged the recorder in at the mains. Forrest winced. Hobson loaded the tape into the machine and pressed the 'play' button. The room was alive with the sound of music.

'Beethoven?' inquired Forrest.

'Yes, sir. Quartet number 13, in B Flat Major.'

'Thank you. I couldn't remember the name of the tune.' He ambled to the door. 'You see, Hobson, I am not as big a lout as you think.'

'Sir, I wouldn't dream of –'

'And I do not regard Beethoven as a serious threat to our security.'

'Thank you, sir.'

'But bloody watch it. Keen-eyed honesty doesn't survive in this climate.'

Forrest left the office. Hobson tidied the cassettes into a briefcase. He would take them home that night. Not all of them were devoted to Beethoven's greatest hits.

In any case, the sweetest music was in the files, and they were securely locked in the boot of his car.

Polling day dawned grey and dank in Northfield Central (South) and the most enthusiastic reception accorded the democratic process was from the staff and students of San Quentin High, which was being used as a polling station, thus giving all the inmates a day's holiday. Long live universal adult suffrage was the prayer on several hundred pairs of lips, as the owners realized they could stay in bed for another hour, or even another day, without fear of penalty.

Jill Swinburne and Trevor Chaplin were exceptions to the horizontal rule. Trevor was driving the van past the Job Centre as Jill addressed the multitude through the loudspeaker, saying: 'A vote for Jill Swinburne is a vote for sanity. A vote for Jill Swinburne is a vote for the English language. A vote for Jill Swinburne is a vote of confidence for the planet Earth.'

'She sounds great, this Jill Swinburne,' said Trevor, 'I think I'll vote for her.'

The candidate switched off the microphone as they hit an early-morning traffic jam caused by road-widening.

'I've now said all that a hundred and fifteen times since breakfast, and it's garbage.'

Trevor urged her on: 'Switch that thing on and get electioneering! George Washington didn't give in by ten o'clock in the morning.'

'He was no sort of conservationist. He practically cleared the world of cherry trees.'

The traffic edged forward and for the one hundred and sixteenth time the voice of Swinburne was heard: 'A vote for Jill Swinburne is a vote for sanity.'

The sound was lost to the queue standing outside the Job Centre as the van drove off towards the Clement Attlee housing estate. There was an additional distraction for the waiting unemployed as Big Al arrived on his bicycle. He dismounted and took from his saddlebag a clip-board and a ball-point pen inscribed: BAY CITY ROLLERS SOUVENIR.

Al knew most of the people in the queue. Many of them were former colleagues from his days on building sites. He strolled along the queue, chatting amiably.

'Morning, Jim. Now then, Alf. How you doing, sunbeam? Anybody fancy striking a blow for freedom? All you have to do is sign an affidavit.'

While Jill Swinburne and Big Al, in their various ways, were fighting for their version of freedom, Sergeant Hobson was pacing the corridors of the town hall, pursuing his own personal battle for self-advancement and, in the light of Forrest's attitude, very likely self-preservation too.

He eventually found the room. It had been reorganized and given its new number, 3887.

'Mr Pitt,' said Hobson, 'you were very helpful to me recently in the matter of the parish church of St Matthew.'

'The basement used as an illicit warehouse? I remember it well. Are there further developments? I have the file close at hand.'

He had several hundred files close at hand. They covered every horizontal surface, and a high proportion of the vertical too.

'No. It concerns one of my files.'

Pitt's face lit up, like a child's on seeing a jumbo cornet with a chocolate flake rampant.

'You have files, sergeant?'

They were blood brothers from that moment on, united in the fraternity of information-gathering.

'I have a file, Mr Pitt, indicating that there has been corruption in the town planning department during the last five years. The corruption involves, among others, a leading Councillor and a well known local businessman.'

'Sounds like the McAllisters.'

'I beg your pardon?'

'I said nothing, sergeant.'

Pitt stared at him, blankly and benignly. Hobson realized there would be no admissions of guilt from this man. He was too spineless to do anything that would justify any worthwhile guilt. The man was meek, dammit, though why such a weed should be officially blessed and guaranteed eventual inheritance of the earth, Hobson could not imagine.

'Mr Pitt, there is no question of your being involved in my investigation. I simply want to talk to you about your predecessor, Mr Anderson.'

'We had a card from him, in Perth, Australia.' Pitt dug into his desk and produced the same brightly-coloured postcard he had shown to Jill. Again he read an abbreviated account of the message on the back: 'He says the weather is very good.' He handed the card to Hobson, inviting him to check its authenticity. 'Do you collect stamps, sergeant?'

Hobson shook his head, and returned the card to Pitt, who restored it to its allotted drawer.

'Tell me about Mr Anderson.'

There was a long silence, while Pitt thought about Mr Anderson, the McAllisters, the processes of law and order, the sunlit beaches of Western Australia and his pension rights. Then he spoke in a voice little more than a whisper: 'Mr Anderson worked at this desk. He cared deeply about the environment. He had lots of good ideas. He had to go. Would you like to see his files?'

'Did Mr Anderson have files?'

Pitt stood up and walked across the room, taking his chair with him. He stood on the chair, and from the top of a tall cupboard lifted down three large box-files, tied round with string. He presented the files to Sergeant Hobson, and whispered: 'Mr Anderson told me there was corruption. I would not listen. He told me, "One day a policeman will walk into this room and start inquiries. When that happens, give him these files." I am giving you the files, Sergeant Hobson, but if challenged I shall deny that I have ever seen you.'

The man's timidity was awesome. Hobson tried to re-assure him: 'A citizen's first duty –'

Pitt finished the statement for him: '– is to protect his job, his superannuation, and his own skin. Local government is the last refuge of the poor in spirit, sergeant. But I have given you the Anderson files, and you must use them as you think fit.'

It was part of Jill's election tactics to drive past the Job Centre at half-hourly intervals. In this way, she calculated, she would be able to convey the gist of her manifesto to the vast majority of the voters in Northfield Central (South).

On one of these circuits, late in the morning, when she and Trevor were debating the possible health hazards of a coffee break at the Golden West Milk Bar, they noticed Big Al in a telephone box at the corner of Ophelia Street.

'Wonder what he's up to?' said Trevor.

'We could stop and ask him.'

'The answer might take hours.'

They drove on.

Had they parked within ten yards of the phone box, they would have heard: 'Sergeant Hobson? Been trying to ring you for the last hour. Would you like some files? I said *files*! You what? Well, suit yourself. I was going to suggest the multi-storey car park. Level four. At noon. I always prefer assignations at noon, don't you?'

He hung up, without waiting for an answer, and returned to the queue outside the Job Centre.

'Come on, lads, last call for affidavits.'

Hobson was surprised when Big Al arrived at level four on his bicycle. Somehow he had imagined that Al would borrow a car for the purpose, but guessed he was being true to some complex proletarian principle.

Al leaned the bicycle carefully against the side of Hobson's car. He removed a dozen bulging files from the saddlebag. He climbed into the car beside the sergeant. 'Files,' he said, piling them on to Hobson.

Hobson leafed through them. They contained a bizarre mixture of handwritten documents and typed sheets, supplemented with occasional cryptic diagrams.

'What are these?'

'Affidavits. There's the case of the money changing hands to get planning permission for a betting shop on our estate. There's the case of the local businessman buying his way off a drunk driving charge. There's the case of the High Street video merchant persuading your Mr Forrest that his dirty movies were actually part of an Open University course on comparative eroticism. There's the –'

Hobson interrupted Al, who was scarcely halfway through the first file. 'Are these authentic cases?'

'As long as you're not too proud to use an odd bit of perjury here and there. I'm quite surprised myself by the high percentage of truth in these files. Anyroad, I'll leave them with you. Would you like some more?'

'Indeed I would!'

'Right little Oliver Twist, aren't you?'

Al climbed out of the car, and remounted his bicycle. He tapped on Hobson's window, indicating he had something to add to the conversation. Hobson wound the window down.

'I feel like the Lone Ranger.'

And Big Al cycled away down the ramp from level four shouting, 'Hi-ho Silver!' at the top of his voice.

Hobson put Al's files in the boot of the car, where they lay snugly alongside Anderson's. He planned to take all of them home where he had already hidden Jill's files in his landlady's deep freeze. On the way he would find a haberdasher's. He needed some pink ribbon.

At nine o'clock that evening, Trevor and Jill climbed into the van. They had eaten a hearty supper of mixed nut salad. Trevor had expected to stay in with a bottle of Frascati, an Ella Fitzgerald album and gentle anticipation. He had forgotten that a day's driving along the length and breadth of the election ward would be followed, inevitably, by the obligatory visit to the town hall, where the votes were being counted, to hail the victor, and smile modestly or bravely, according to the result.

As they drove away from the house, Trevor giggled.

'What's funny?'

'We should have left a note on the door saying we're out for the count.'

There was no need to leave a note. The Jaguar was parked opposite the house. The man in dark glasses was watching. He had seen them go. He knew they were out for the count.

It was a record turn-out in Northfield Central (South). The poll was seventeen per cent, the lowest ever recorded, even in an area where revolutionary fervour had long since been swamped by Woodbines and draught bitter, and the major public debates concerned the relative merits of *Dallas* and *Dynasty*.

Trevor was disappointed when he saw the interior of the town hall. Where were the long rows of tables? Where was the feverish excitement? Where were the commentators and pundits and pollsters he had seen on television coverage of by-elections? Where were the crowds of supporters of the rival parties, with their rossettes and cheers and counter-cheers? Not here. Not tonight.

The electorate was represented by Big Al, who greeted

them with a stolid assessment: 'My information is a land-slide victory for the don't-knows, don't-cares, and don't-give-a-buggers. Sorry, flower.'

Before Jill could respond, the returning officer blew into the microphone on stage and asked for the candidates.

'The moment of truth,' said Jill.

'There's only three possibilities. Win, lose or draw,' said Al.

Trevor smiled with what he intended to be encouragement: 'And to us you'll always be the winner.'

'Bollocks.'

They watched as Jill crossed the floor of the town hall towards the stage, a tiny figure in a vast arena, designed for housing Handel's *Messiah*, but now empty of chairs.

Trevor and Al were concentrating so hard on the major political event about to take place on the platform that they did not hear Sergeant Hobson approaching from the back of the hall. He tapped them on the shoulder.

'Good heavens,' said Al, 'a formidable police presence.'

'I thought I should warn you,' said Hobson, speaking with quiet urgency, 'things are warming up. Be careful. The chickens are coming home to roost.'

He left as surreptitiously as he had arrived.

'What was all that about?' said Trevor.

'Chickens,' said Al, and turned to face the stage.

Jill stood in a line with the other three candidates, all of them men, representing the Conservative Party, the Labour Party and the Alliance. They were, respectively, an insurance broker, a polytechnic lecturer and a dentist. Without their rosettes, it would have been difficult to tell one from another.

The returning officer announced the votes cast: 'Carstairs, Conservative, 629 votes ... Maddox, Labour, 627 votes ... Bradshaw, Alliance, 624 votes ... Swinburne, Conservation, 54 votes.'

Jill won the moral victory. She marched across the stage, took the microphone from the returning officer, and cried: 'I demand a recount!' Then she shook hands with the other candidates, wished them well for the recount, left the stage, crossed the floor to re-join Trevor and Al and said: 'Let's go home.'

Al, as usual, had some other business to attend to, and declined the invitation to join them at Jill's for fish and chips and a bottle of cheap wine. He cycled away into the darkness.

'Have we got any cheap wine?' asked Jill.

'There's a bottle of Chianti at the flat.'

'Perfect. I fancy waking up with a headache, don't you?'

As they were climbing into the van, Trevor noticed a Jaguar parked across the road. It seemed familiar.

'I've seen that car before.'

'All cars look alike to me,' said Jill.

As Hobson drove fast through the night to a large, detached house on the very edges of Harrogate itself, he was talking to himself: 'There is a tide in the affairs of men, which, taken at the flood, leads on to the home of the chief constable at ten-thirty on a dank Thursday evening, with a mighty cargo of incriminating evidence, all tied up in pink ribbon.'

He whistled a few bars of 'The Dambusters' March', then, as the rain started to fall and he had to start the wipers on their rhythmic way, he picked up the metre of their movement with the words: 'Cry God for Hobson, England and St George!'

Trevor ran up the stairs leading to his flat. He knew that Al and Norm had removed most of the refrigerators and gas cookers earlier in the day, and was very confident of finding the bottle of Chianti in its proper place: on the bookshelf between Derek Jewell's life of Duke Ellington and Duke Ellington's life of Duke Ellington.

He did not expect to find his flat wrecked. Drawers pulled out and tipped on the floor: crockery smashed, books and papers ploughed and scattered: his posters of Charlie Parker, Lester Young, King Oliver and Billie Holiday ripped from their hangers and shredded. Had not these four paid a big enough price in blood during their lifetime? Would they never be left alone?

Records had been taken from the sleeves and hurled across the room. Trevor dared not look at them closely. He was happy to find the bottle of Chianti intact, to lock the door on the carnage and get the Hell out.

Jill's house had received the same treatment. She and Trevor sat among the debris, eating their fish and chips and drinking wine from the bottle. Like the people who sang 'Bless 'Em All' in the air-raid shelters during the Blitz, they were totally united in fiendish adversity. They passed the wine back and forth, and did not even consider wiping the bottle before drinking.

'I wonder who they were,' said Jill.

'The McAllisters. That's who did it.'

'Not this. The fifty-four people who voted for me.'

'I was one.'

'Thank you, Trevor.'

She finished her fish and chips, rolled up the paper in a ball and flung it across the room. One more item of garbage made little difference to the scene of devastation around them.

'Hang spring-cleaning!' she said.

'Pardon?'

'It's from *The Wind in the Willows*. Ratty and Mole are supposed to be spring-cleaning, but they get really pissed off and they say, "Hang spring-cleaning!" and they mess about on the river instead.'

Trevor stood up and crossed to the window. He stared into the darkness, as if calculating the direction of the nearest navigable river. 'Not so sure about rivers. I don't swim very well. We could take to the hills.' He pointed into the blackness beyond the pouring rain. 'See? The Yorkshire Dales.'

Jill joined him at the window, to have a look at the Yorkshire Dales. Though it was dark and stormy, she could see them clearly.

'When? The weekend?'

'We could go tomorrow,' said Trevor.

'What about school?'

'We'll think of a silly excuse. A plague of locusts. Or we'll say your house has been struck by a thunderbolt. Which is more or less true.'

She looked at him, nose to nose.

'Thank you, Trevor.'

He put his arms around her. She put her arms around him. They kissed gently. He giggled.

'What's funny?'

'Have you ever noticed how spiders get trapped in your double-glazing?'

She hit him, nicely.

Next day, Trevor Chaplin and Jill Swinburne ran away into the hills.

Mr Carter did not run away into the hills. He strolled along to the headmaster's study to report their absence.

'But this renders my timetable into tattered shreds of wastepaper,' said Mr Wheeler. 'Are they ill?'

'Mrs Swinburne has apparently had a recurrence of inherited malaria. I didn't know this, but it seems her father was a district officer in the colonies, when there were such things.'

'And Mr Chaplin?'

Mr Carter hesitated, not out of trepidation, but because he relished any legitimate excuse to irritate his headmaster.

'It was a rather bad line, and Mr Chaplin does tend to mumble, but it sounded like ... a touch of the PMTs.'

The headmaster absorbed this news slowly, building up a head of highly toxic steam.

'You realize, Mr Carter, that further education cuts are threatened and we may well be faced with the question of compulsory redundancies at the end of term.'

Mr Carter beamed across the desk: 'May I say, head-master, that I would welcome redundancy with open arms, if it were accompanied by an appropriate cash settlement. Used notes, if possible.'

Superintendent Forrest did not run away into the hills. He walked quietly along the corridor to the door that now bore the handwritten legend: THE EARL OF HOBSON, BA. He went in. Hobson stood up smartly, to attention.

'Stand easy, Hobson,' said Forrest, who had found the young detective's quasi-military habits irritating in the beginning but had warmed to them recently for reasons he could not begin to identify. 'Hobson. Do you know where sir is going in half an hour's time?'

'No, sir.'

'Sir has been summoned for an interview with the chief constable.'

'I see.'

'Do you have the remotest idea why sir has been summoned in this way?'

'I do have a remote idea, sir.'

'Sit down, Hobson, for God's sake.'

The two men sat down, either side of the desk. It was a pointed reversal of their first meeting. Hobson sat behind the desk, in the conventional position of authority.

'It's amazing, Hobson, really amazing. I tell you to stop fiddling with buttons and catch a thief, and the first time you do it, it's me that gets nicked.'

'Bang to rights, sir, unless I'm very much mistaken.'

'Exactly.'

They both sensed a small ripple of trust, even friendship, lapping the edges of their relationship. Forrest was asking for help. He was sitting on the proper side of the desk.

'Hobson. Give me your advice, as a graduate copper, and embodiment of the shape of things to come.'

'Anything I can do, sir . . .'

'I am right in it, up to my shell-likes. What is your advice?'

'I should hire the best criminal lawyer that you can afford. Fight information with information.'

'I'm glad we see eye to eye on that, Hobson.' Forrest stood up and crossed to the door. 'Well done, son. I like to see my lads doing well.'

Two minutes after Forrest left, the door opened and in walked Joe and Ben, with sincere congratulations and a bundle of files which they placed reverentially on Hobson's desk.

'What's all this?' asked Hobson.

'Files,' said Joe.

'More evidence against Mr Forrest,' added Ben.

Hobson, who had begun to feel a growing compassion for his superintendent, a compassion that grated against his sense of justice, opened the first file.

'All good stuff,' said Joe, 'satisfaction guaranteed. We just want to maintain the English tradition.'

'Which English tradition?'

'Self-preservation. Always kick a man when he's down.'

'That isn't the English tradition.'

'Where have you been the last twenty years?' said Joe and Ben in unison. They had been practising.

Dave Jordan, star presenter on Swaledale Sound, the commercial radio station that transmitted Golden Oldies twenty-four hours a day up to a radius of thirty miles from his sound-proof, windowless cubicle deep in a converted mill, had not run away into the hills. He was just playing Ringo Starr singing 'When I'm Sixty-Four' to celebrate an old lady's seventy-ninth birthday, to be followed by a commercial for the Golden West Milk Bar, when he was handed a newsflash, which he read in his characteristic mid-Atlantic accent with pastel shades of Hunslet.

'It has been confirmed that a major inquiry is going on into allegations of corruption in the police force and local government. A senior police officer has been suspended and also assisting in the inquiries are a well known local businessman and a city Councillor and member of the planning committee.'

There were sixty-five transistor radios stored in Big Al's shed at the Tolpuddle Street allotments. Four of them were switched on at the time of the newsflash, part of a continuing experiment Al was conducting into quadra-phonic sound.

'It only works if you've got four ears,' he announced to Norm, who had perked up at the newsflash.

'Hey, we did that, didn't we? With our affidavits.'

'We no doubt played a part in the apprehension of the malefactors, Norm.'

Al was staring thoughtfully at a row of twelve kettles, trying to decide which one to use to make a cup of tea.

'A lot of them was true, them affidavits,' said Norm,

losing his grasp of syntax in his enthusiasm. 'All that corruption and taking bribes and backhanders.'

'Never mind corruption,' said Big Al. 'Smashing up a greenhouse. That's the cardinal sin.'

Trevor Chaplin and Jill Swinburne really had run away into the hills. They had no idea which hills. Trevor had driven without compass or AA book, dead reckoning. They might have been in Airedale or Wharfedale, Swaledale or Nidderdale. It mattered not. They had found the sun, and a warm breeze, and the good earth.

They parked the car at the top of a hill and stared out across the landscape.

'Whyebuggerman!' murmured Trevor. It said everything.

They ran down the hill in simulated slow motion, pretending they were in a Truffaut film. At the foot of the hill they circled each other slowly and tenderly, fingertips touching, singing the theme from *Love Story*.

They climbed the hill, puffing and panting, then sat on a rock to recover.

'You are right,' said Jill. 'Whyebuggerman!'

Trevor laughed at her accent.

'I like it when we hang spring-cleaning. I might do it every day.'

They realized dimly that Sergeant Hobson was probably arresting the highest and mightiest in the land, that the rich and well born might be walking in single file around the exercise yard of the nearest open prison. It seemed trivial and unimportant. Today was about Jill Swinburne and Trevor Chaplin, in either order.

'The silly thing is,' said Jill, 'we got together because my marriage broke up and you started giving me lifts to school and I never expected it would become important.'

'And is it?'

'Yes. It's important.'

Another silence, gently tinted with bird song, with breeze, with the sounds of sheep, all so sharp they could have been sound effects, dubbed on by a romantic sound engineer.

Trevor looked at her, realizing how important this woman had become to him, with her healthy food and overpowering concern for the planet Earth.

'I sometimes wonder whether I should say . . . will you marry me?'

'You won't say that, will you, Mr Chaplin?'

'Oh no,' he said hastily.

'I am Jill Swinburne. You are Trevor Chaplin.'

'We are us.'

Another long silence, rich with contentment and trust. Then, on a secret sign from somewhere deep in the hills, it was time to move on. They stood up, side by side, not touching.

'Let's go somewhere and be us,' said Jill.

'Righto, pet,' said Trevor.

BARRY WOODWARD

Brookside One: **Changing Lives**

Overnight, one madman with a gun brought dramatic change to the lives of Brookside's residents. Every household in the Close – young and old – was shocked by the shooting of black nurse Kate Moses.

Nevertheless life has to go on . . .

As, week by week, the memories of the siege at Brookside fade, those left behind have other problems and choices to face.

KATHLEEN POTTER

Brookside Two: **Weathering the Storm**

A summer wedding for Heather, and a second chance –
but all is not what it seems. Nick has a secret, and
Heather has difficulty with her step-children. Across
the close the Grants have to come to terms with an
attack on Sheila, and the list of suspects causes uncom-
fortable reverberations in some unlikely corners of
Brookside Close. Rod comes of age in style, and needs
all his resilience and resourcefulness as he plans his
future in present-day Merseyside . . .

As temperatures rise and the days grow longer, turmoil
is never far away for the inhabitants of the Close, with
secrets to be hidden and new problems to be
confronted.

JOHN BURKE

King & Castle

Ronald King is a bent copper whose dirty dealings are catching up with him, and who has to quit the Met before it quits him.

David Castle is a gentle but tough aikido teacher and part-time genealogist, with debts to pay, a custody case to fight . . . and no steady income.

Thrown together by circumstance and desperation, these two join forces as King & Castle, Debt Collectors. From the East End to Wimbledon, the pair tread the fine line dividing law from disorder. They're the most diverting duo since Arthur Daley and Terry McCann.

JOHN BURKE

The Bill

Wapping, in the East End of London, is a tough
manor. A typical day has dippers in the High Street,
break-ins to cars and homes, lost dogs and runaway
kids. The patch has its fair share of more serious crime
too – drugs, armed robbery, porn. For PC Carver,
fresh from Hendon, Sergeant Cryer, Detective Inspector Galloway and the rest of the Bill based at Sun Hill
Police Station, there is no respite. And the not-always-
friendly rivalry between uniformed and plain-clothes
branches does little to ease the tension . . .

Top Fiction from Methuen Paperbacks

While every effort is made to keep prices low, it is sometimes necessary to increase prices at short notice. Methuen Paperbacks reserves the right to show new retail prices on covers which may differ from those previously advertised in the text or elsewhere.

The prices shown below were correct at the time of going to press.

☐ 413 55810 X	**Lords of the Earth**	Patrick Anderson	£2.95
☐ 417 02530 0	**Little Big Man**	Thomas Berger	£2.50
☐ 417 04830 0	**Life at the Top**	John Braine	£1.95
☐ 413 57370 2	**The Two of Us**	John Braine	£1.95
☐ 417 02100 3	**Waiting for Sheila**	John Braine	£1.95
☐ 417 05360 6	**The Good Earth**	Pearl S Buck	£1.95
☐ 417 05810 1	**Man of Nazareth**	Anthony Burgess	£1.50
☐ 413 57930 1	**Here Today**	Zoë Fairbairns	£1.95
☐ 413 58680 4	**Dominator**	James Follett	£2.50
☐ 417 03890 9	**The Rich and the Beautiful**	Ruth Harris	£1.75
☐ 417 04590 5	**Sometimes a Great Notion**	Ken Kesey	£2.95
☐ 413 55620 4	**Second from Last in the Sack Race**	David Nobbs	£2.50
☐ 413 52370 5	**Titus Groan**	Mervyn Peake	£2.50
☐ 413 52350 0	**Gormenghast**	Mervyn Peake	£2.50
☐ 413 52360 8	**Titus Alone**	Mervyn Peake	£1.95
☐ 417 05390 8	**Lust for Life**	Irving Stone	£1.95
☐ 413 53790 0	**The Secret Diary of Adrian Mole Aged 13¾**	Sue Townsend	£1.95
☐ 413 58810 6	**The Growing Pains of Adrian Mole**	Sue Townsend	£1.95
☐ 413 58060 1	**The Set-Up**	Vladimir Volkoff	£2.50
☐ 413 55570 4	**Charlie**	Nigel Williams	£1.95

All these books are available at your bookshop or newsagent, or can be ordered direct from the publisher. Just tick the titles you want and fill in the form below.

Methuen Paperbacks, Cash Sales Department,
PO Box 11, Falmouth,
Cornwall TR10 109EN.

Please send cheque or postal order, no currency, for purchase price quoted and allow the following for postage and packing:

UK	55p for the first book, 22p for the second book and 14p for each additional book ordered to a maximum charge of £1.75.
BFPO and Eire	55p for the first book, 22p for the second book and 14p for each next seven books, thereafter 8p per book.
Overseas Customers	£1.00 for the first book plus 25p per copy for each additional book.

NAME (Block Letters) ....

ADDRESS...

....